Mission to Marseilles

Léo Malet was born in Montpellier in 1909. He had no formal education and began as a cabaret singer at 'La Vache enragée' in Montmartre in 1925. He became an anarchist and contributed to various magazines: *L'Insurgé, Le Journal de l'Homme aux Sandales* . . . He had a variety of jobs: office worker, ghost writer, manager of a fashion magazine, cinema extra, newspaper seller . . .

From 1930 to 1940 he belonged to the Surrealist Group and was a close friend of André Breton, René Magritte, and Yves Tanguy. During that time he published several collections of poetry.

In 1943, inspired by the American writers Raymond Chandler and Dashiel Hammett, he created Nestor Burma, the Parisian private detective whose first mystery *120 rue de la Gare* was an instant success and marked the beginning of a new era in French detective fiction.

More than sixty novels were to follow over the next twenty years. Léo Malet won the 'Grand Prix de la Littérature policière' in 1947 and the 'Grand Prix de l'Humour noir' in 1958 for his series 'Les Nouveaux Mystères de Paris', each of which is set in a different *arrondissement*.

Mission to Marseilles (*Le Cinquième Procédé*) is set in wartime France and was first published in 1947.

Léo Malet lives in Châtillon, just south of Paris.

D1313218

Léo Malet

Mission to Marseilles

translated from the French by Olive Classe
general editor: Barbara Bray

Pan Books
London, Sydney and Auckland

First published in France 1947 by S.E.P.E., Paris,
under the title *Le Cinquième Procédé*

This edition first published in Great Britain 1991 by
Pan Books Ltd, Cavaye Place, London SW10 9PG

9 8 7 6 5 4 3 2 1

ISBN 0 330 31849 7

Typeset by Macmillan Production Limited

Printed in England by Clays Ltd, St Ives plc

to Jean Rougeul

Contents

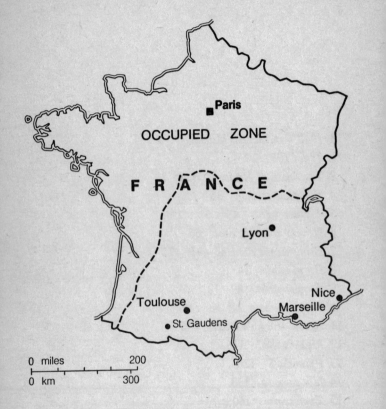

1 1942 – *mission in Marseilles*

Jackie Lamour – love by name and love by nature – was a sight worth going a long way to see.

It was almost entirely because of her sex appeal that I'd made the journey from Paris to Marseilles. There, at the Blackbird Club in the rue Vacon, she was delighting an audience of 'refugees' from the Occupied Zone.

She'd lifted an idea from Jean Cocteau (I later discovered he too was a kind of illusionist) and was dancing in a dark leotard in front of a black curtain, so that all you could see were her head and legs moving about. A sort of 'sawing a woman in half' effect. But the half that survived was quite enough to keep the audience agog: those legs were really something. And one evening, lucky devil that I am, I got to see those invisible but no less irresistible arms. Fragrant, provocative, shapely, they were in a class of their own. The left one, though, had a slight blemish about four inches above the elbow: a scar that couldn't have been made by an admirer throwing a bouquet. I only got a quick impression – it wasn't a moment for hanging about – but it looked very much like an old bullet wound.

*

Robert Beaucher had said the things he wanted back were probably either in the desk or in the drawer of a little table by the piano. Jackie was no fool: she knew there was much to be said for hiding things in obvious places.

But sharing Jackie's bed had given Beaucher delusions about her brains. The object of my search was in neither of the places he'd suggested. But I kept looking and finally found it among some papers on the top shelf of a bookcase. All this poking around had taken time, and I was just about to withdraw, pleased at having done what I'd come to do without rousing the flunkey who slept on the top floor, when I heard the sound of a car approaching. It stopped outside the house before I could make a getaway.

Surely it was too early for Jackie to be coming back from the night-club? I ran and opened a front window. Two people were crunching along the gravel drive, and I could hear a muffled conversation, partly drowned by the noise of the engine still running out on the road.

I was wrong – it *was* the dancer: the man with her was calling her Jackie, and she was snuffling about how draughty the Blackbird's dressing-rooms were. She'd caught a cold – that must be it – cancelled her act and come home early.

The man seemed genuinely sorry about this, but more on his own account than on hers. At first I thought my searches in the chilly drawing-room had affected my hearing – even in Marseilles November's still November. In the end, though, I had to face the fact: I knew this joker's voice. It was funny really. In a way.

They came into the house, and I heard doors opening and shutting and Jackie saying there was no need to wake

Joseph. (If she went on making that racket Joseph would be leaping out of bed of his own accord.) The man agreed, then said that something or other had to be settled once and for all.

'You must be out of your mind!' she snapped. Robert Beaucher had been right. Jackie Lamour was a tough cookie.

They finally came into the next room: I could hear them trying to light the stove. I applied my ear to the communicating door. Jackie was still moaning on about her cold and the boss of the Blackbird. Every so often, by way of a change, she had a go at her companion. According to her he was a complete dope at lighting fires, and he and his rotten car, which kept stopping every ten yards, made a good pair. The dope didn't answer. He must be having a laugh to himself on the quiet, thought I. After I'd listened for a bit I reckoned I'd better clear out before the two lovebirds decided to come and make music in my drawing-room.

But the layout of the place was such that they were now obstructing my escape route. As I couldn't leave by the door I'd have to fall back on the windows. There I met with a disappointment. The shutters were firmly padlocked, and as for forcing them, not a hope. I had a try, but soon saw it was no good.

I obviously wasn't going to be able to conceal my presence, so with the tools that had proved useless on the shutters I decided to do a bit of damage elsewhere – some drawers and the lock of a safe – to make my visit look like an ordinary burglary. The safe contained a number of banknotes and some earrings. I pocketed the lot.

Putting away my torch, I buttoned my coat, pulled my muffler over my mouth and my hat down over my eyes, then took out my revolver. I listened at the door long enough to hear the sniffling of La Lamour, the roar of the stove that the dope had finally got going, and a few mumbled words from the dope himself. Then I turned the knob, gave the door an almighty kick, and appeared on the threshold like the demon king.

Jackie was so stunned she couldn't utter a sound. As for her companion, he reached for the ceiling without waiting to be told. I knew he wouldn't put up any resistance in spite of his bulk.

'Hands up and keep quiet!' I barked in a voice that sounded as though it meant business.

The dancer, more and more flabbergasted, obeyed. And it was then, as the ample sleeve of her négligé slipped back, that I saw the scar.

The shock was making her bosom heave. And – another feature not vouchsafed the clients of the Blackbird Club despite their drinks at 75 francs a go – peeping through the lace was one of the prettiest, firmest little breasts you ever could wish to see.

Even so, I couldn't stand about as if I was waiting for Madame Pétain to have quins. This beauty queen was too quick on the uptake. Once the surprise had worn off she'd soon work out that there was only one of me.

I didn't give her the chance. Stepping swiftly into the room I dealt her a single tap on the head with my revolver butt. She slumped on to the bed. I laid a cushion over her head to assist her breathing, then went over to the chap. I put a finger to my lips, gave a significant pat to the pocket where I'd put my swag, made a vague gesture of apology, then let him have *his* share. He rolled with the punch, but that didn't prevent him from staggering back as if he'd stopped it. He hit the wall and dropped to the ground, managing as he fell to connect with a corner of the furniture. His aquiline nose began to spurt like a fountain. Well, I thought, if this guy ever goes bankrupt he can always try the stage. There couldn't be many as good at faking as he was.

Leaving both of them dead to the world, I slipped out of the bedroom and into the hall, where I stood and listened. Our little set-to hadn't been all that noisy. Joseph was still asleep upstairs.

I opened the front door with the duplicate keys that had let me into the house and, still without making a sound, double-locked it behind me. It was distinctly chilly outside. The pine trees were sighing in the wind from the sea.

Extracting a hammer and chisel from the boot of the car, I went back and wrecked the lock of the door into the kitchen, to make it look as if I'd got in that way.

Then I climbed behind the wheel of the car – the engine was still running – and headed for Marseilles.

I got there without a hitch, despite Jackie's acid remarks about breakdowns. The streets were deserted. I prayed I wouldn't meet a police patrol, and must have been in God's good books as I didn't see any sign of a cop. So I parked the car in front of a certain house and walked back to my hotel.

A nearby clock was striking one as I went into my room. For an hour it had been the 8th of November – the 8th of November 1942. Already, over on the other side of the Mediterranean, some of the boys in Algiers were starting to feel nervous. Those who knew about the American landing.

*

Six hours later I was still awake when a phone call came for me.

'Why haven't you brought me my property?' snarled Robert Boucher.

'I was waiting for you to ring me.'

'Well, now I have!'

'Right. I'll be with you straight away.'

'Hold on a minute . . . '

The night's events seemed to have left him in some confusion. He told me not to come at once and especially not to come to his place. We finally arranged to meet at ten o'clock in the Vieux Port. I listened patiently to his instructions until he told me to proceed with the greatest caution. Then I retorted that he had cause to know I always proceeded with caution, and hung up. I took the bundle of letters I'd recovered from the dancer's villa and wrapped it in a newspaper. I made a second parcel of the banknotes and jewellery I'd lifted to conceal the real purpose of my visit. Then, intending to return to Paris that evening – I'd had enough of the Unoccupied Zone – I packed my bags and put them by the bed, except for a leather briefcase which I left in the hotel safe.

When I went out the streets were buzzing with excitement. News of the Allied operation in North Africa had just come through and was causing a great sensation, especially as it was a Sunday. Obvious strangers were talking to one another. Fabrication flourished. The names of Pétain, Darlan, Noguès and Roosevelt were flying around. I bought a special edition and went to a café to wait until the time of my appointment. It was a quiet place where they couldn't care less about current events so long as they didn't affect the black market. The speciality of the house was real coffee. After three cups I felt restored. I needed to be. I'd want all my wits about me when I checked my fee.

Robert Beaucher had arranged to meet me in an odd sort of dive. The woman who opened the door was a peroxide blonde wearing a kimono past its first bloom over a body in a similar state. Eyes dull with fatigue gave me a nasty look. Her hair and make-up were in urgent need of first aid and intensive care respectively. In short, she had all the attributes of a madam first thing in the morning.

Looking at her, I decided my client was a hopeless case. If he didn't cut down on debauchery he'd be singing like Caruso for the rest of his life. Having Jackie Lamour dealt with wouldn't solve the problem. Still, it was nothing to do with me. If there were no mugs like him about, blackmailers and private detectives would all have to work in factories. The very thought brought my hands out in blisters.

It was just on ten o'clock, but Beaucher hadn't come yet. The old girl showed me into a windowless room lit by one anaemic bulb, a sort of 'Japanese' salon that in days before it got so dusty must have resounded to the laughter and oaths of the seafaring fraternity. I sat down, smoked my pipe and pondered.

Robert Beaucher, industrialist, was certainly a queer fish. When he first saw me he looked as if he was going to have a fit. Then all the time we were talking he seemed very tickled. True, I might have looked rather odd. I was wearing a trenchcoat, plus-fours, a trilby hat and a moustache. It was probably the moustache he found so hilarious: it made me look more like an ordinary rozzer than an elegant private eye à la Peter Wimsey.

Every so often I used to take a notion to grow a

moustache, partly out of laziness and partly with the pious intention of looking like my father. According to his photographs he wore great handlebars guaranteed to attract flocks of admiring females. But women's tastes have changed since then. My soup-strainer, assumed in the line of business, wasn't at all to the liking of Hélène Chatelain, my secretary. And it had only made my client laugh.

At that point in my ruminations he finally turned up. He wasn't laughing now. His nose still bore the marks of its encounter with the furniture, and he seemed edgy and out of temper. Perhaps he had political objections to the American landing.

'Well?' he snapped without preamble. 'Have you got the letters?'

'Here.'

He nearly snatched the packet of love letters out of my hands, then undid the black ribbon that tied them together and began to count them feverishly.

'They're all there,' I said. 'Seventeen of them. As you said. I didn't know,' I added, 'that you called yourself Peter. A nice pseudonym for a lover, Peter . . . as in Ibbetson.'

He frowned.

'Do you mean to say you've read them?'

I almost admitted I had, and that they'd given me a good laugh, but I thought it best to offer a professional explanation: I'd been obliged to take the elementary precaution of checking the nature of the documents. I couldn't risk going off with the ravings of some other loony.

'Fair enough,' he said. But he didn't sound too sure.

I reminded him that a private detective is practically the same as a priest.

'Maybe,' he said shortly.

Anyhow he stowed the packet away in his overcoat pocket and gave me my money. In cash – much more convenient than a cheque. When I'd counted it I enquired after the lady, and wasn't surprised to learn that as soon as she woke up, so to speak, she'd kicked up a shindy.

'But no bones broken, I hope?'

'Just a bump, that's all.'

'And what about you?'

'I'm all right,' he growled.

'It was difficult to avoid hurting you.'

'Yes, I could see that straight away.'

I laughed. 'You put on a very good act. Anyone not in the know would have thought I was Primo Carnera . . . Just the same, our operation didn't exactly pass unnoticed! What tough luck that this dame, who's been waving her legs in the breeze for months, should wait to catch cold till the very night we needed her to come home late! . . . It could have been a real fiasco . . . A good thing you decided to spend the evening negotiating with her,' I added artlessly, 'and incidentally giving yourself an alibi.'

'Spare me your conjectures,' he interrupted sourly. He clearly didn't like me going into the whys and wherefores. But that's my trade, and I didn't give a hang about his feelings now I'd been paid.

'If she'd come home in her own car I mightn't have had time to finish the job. I was just getting ready to leave when you both turned up. I take it you did all you could to prolong the journey – making out the car kept breaking down and all that. I saw later on there was nothing wrong with it. Sorry I had to leave you without transport, but I needed to get away from the scene of the crime as fast as possible. Anyhow, here are the keys you lent me, and

17

the things I took from the safe – you'll need to work out some way of getting them back to her. Incidentally, did she notice the letters had gone?'

'I don't think so,' said Beaucher. 'The break-in threw her completely.'

'She'll be reporting it to the police, I suppose?'

'Er . . . yes . . . I suppose so . . . '

'She hasn't called them in yet?'

'She hadn't when I left her.'

'Well, fix it so that she has her property back first. I'd rather the matter didn't go any further.'

He didn't answer, but he put the things I'd stolen in his pocket and indicated the interview was over. I'd sensed that this conversation was getting on his nerves, and I myself was dying for some fresh air. So when he made for the door, I followed.

'I'd be obliged if you'd wait here another quarter of an hour,' he said, stopping me. 'It's better we shouldn't be seen together.'

I laughed at his cowardice. 'Jackie can't do you any harm now you've got the letters,' I said. 'And anyway I don't suppose she's hovering around outside . . . Still, just as you like.'

I sat down. As it happened, I dozed off, and didn't leave till more like half an hour after he did. By some miracle the old girl remembered me languishing in the 'Japanese' room and came and woke me up.

I strolled around for a bit and then, catching sight of myself in a mirror, debated whether to shave off my moustache. Getting rid of it would wake me up properly. Naturally, there was no question of doing it myself. Too much of an effort. I tried several barber's shops but they were crowded. So I gave up the idea and went to the Gare St Charles to find out about the times of the trains to Paris. The booking clerk sardonically recommended train 108 at 19.00 hours: the only one there was.

I went back to the hotel for a bit of a nap. It was the best I could do in the circumstances.

2 Train 108

There were seven of us in the compartment. The ceiling light was dimmed, for black-out purposes only. Nobody, alas, was thinking of going to sleep. There was one other silent passenger besides myself, but the other five never stopped jawing about the landing. This event was beginning to get on my wick. For some while I sat there being bored stiff, but when I realized the subject might well see us through to the next world war I told them in no uncertain terms to change the blasted record. They glared back furiously, assuming my political opinions must be the direct opposite of theirs. So then there was a right royal row, in which a belligerent female played a leading role.

When that had more or less died down, off they went again about the landing, so I moved my luggage to the end of the coach, where I'd noticed an empty seat.

I didn't know how the vamp sitting opposite felt about the new Europe, but whatever her convictions I was prepared to fall in with them. The arguments in favour of conversion were a pair of legs shapely enough to give Jackie Lamour varicose veins at the sight. The owner of these powerful persuaders also had a very pretty face, in the beautiful blonde spy style which I don't dislike at all. No need to draw a diagram: I began to chat her up, leading the conversation on to – can't you guess – the Allied landing. She shot me a pitying glance for my lack of originality. Still, now and again she would give a faint smile. It took me an hour to realize it was my moustache that was amusing her. At that point I nearly stuck it in her kisser, as the train jerked to a halt with much clanking and hissing. We were at Chalon-sur-Saône. We started to hunt out our papers and identity cards, ready to cross the demarcation line.

The door slid open to admit a young *Wehrmacht* officer accompanied by a girl in uniform, quite slim for a German. He stamped my fellow passenger's papers after only a cursory glance; but did he take his time over me! My occupation of 'private detective' must have looked suspicious. He examined my documents in the utmost detail, pausing sometimes to throw me an appraising look or show something to his colleague. After ten minutes' scrutiny of my pass, he finally handed me back my papers with an almost friendly nod. The girl was smiling too. As they walked away, I heard him jabbering something about *Polizisten* and *Brüder*. Just because I was a detective this specimen took me for a 'brother'. No chance!

After this incident my fair companion looked at me with rather more interest, and when the train moved off again I continued my stalking tactics, still noting the mocking smile she wore as she eyed my moustache. Suddenly I could stand it no longer. Taking my razor with me, I went off to the loo the whip off my whiskers. When I got back to the compartment, it boasted a couple more occupants. The younger of the two had taken up where I'd left off and was already telling the vamp the tale. She didn't deign to notice the change in my appearance. I sat down.

'We're stopping again,' said the young man. The train was losing speed.

'No,' replied the other newcomer, an old boy with a goatee. 'We must be at La Haute-Futaie. They're repairing the track – it seems to be going on for ever. They've been at it for months, and the trains always slow down here for a good half mile . . . '

By now we were going at practically walking pace.

'Some express train, if you'll pardon the express-ion,' joked the young man, scoring a load of points with our fair companion, if you can believe it.

I decided to have a doze.

When we drew into the Gare de Lyon the huge station clock was getting ready to strike ten. I shook myself awake, mouth dry and limbs aching. For the hundred-thousandth time since 1939 I cursed the war. Among other things it made the trains go all round the houses.

Under the great sooty glass roof the light was murky. I got my baggage together and joined the drowsy crowd swarming along the platform. I'd just got to the head of the train when the stream of passengers halted, and I saw the stationmaster, followed by two uniformed cops, hurrying towards one of the coaches. He had a look on his face that aroused my interest. I turned and followed.

A policeman seemed to be trying to stop anyone from getting into the part of the train where I'd been sitting. I walked past him and got on farther back, where there was no one checking. There were people blocking the corridor. I went up and stuck my head between those of two other busybodies, but all I could see was four people, including a uniformed policeman, bending over something on the floor in one of the compartments. Beside them, his face twitching violently, stood the stationmaster. Suddenly I heard a woman's voice telling someone called Jules, 'It's that rude man who got on at Marseilles.' I craned my neck a bit and who did I find in front of me but the harridan I'd given a rocket to the previous night, the one who'd been driving me dotty with her Allied landing. She had her back to me, but presumably, from what she said, she must have seen me.

'Well, what of it?' I cried. 'Have you booked all the seats for this show? Aren't I allowed to look too?'

Everybody was surprised to hear me raising my voice, but the old hag herself broke all records. She whirled round as if a snake had bitten her. She was pale already, but now she went whiter still. 'His moustache!' she croaked; and then passed out. Another one who must have been impressed by my face-fungus. Beginning to get a sniff of something peculiar, I stepped forward. The man Jules grabbed my arm.

'Don't try to get away!'

'I've no intention of doing so,' I replied.

He only tightened his grip. Then he asked where my moustache was, telling everyone I'd had one when we left Marseilles but must have shaved it off during the journey. He appended various remarks about my manners, my politics, and how I'd upset his wife.

He was cut short by a man who emerged from the compartment chewing his lip. The stiff collar, double-breasted jacket and striped trousers dusty at the knees all betokened a railway police official. He looked at me apprehensively and asked: '*Did* you have a moustache? Why did you get rid of it?'

'D'you need a permit from the German High Command these days, then?'

To make his eyes pop right out of their sockets I thought I'd explain about the attitude of the beautiful blonde spy, but I bit it back. The other people in the compartment had moved aside, and now, edging forward a bit, I saw . . .

Wherever this passenger had presented his *Ausweis* to cross the line between life and death, he'd been let through with no questions asked, judging by the amount of blood. But that wasn't all. He was wearing a grubby trenchcoat, golfing trousers and a brown trilby. All exactly like mine. And his upper lip was adorned with a splendid moustache.

If I'd ever had a brother, that's what he'd have looked like.

Only approximately, though: the resemblance was more superficial than real. Nothing looks more like a trench-coat than another trenchcoat, especially if they both require the services of a dry-cleaner. And two brown trilbies can easily be mistaken for each other. Likewise plus-fours. Apart from these similarities, and the famous moustache, our faces differed markedly, the dead man's being heavier and broader than mine. Our haircuts too were completely different. Only someone who didn't know me well could have confused me with the corpse. Like the harridan, who was now gradually coming to.

'I'm not exactly his double, even with a moustache,' I said to the Superintendent, jerking my chin towards the stiff stretched out between the two seats.

I pointed out the differences.

'You've got your wits about you,' he said suspiciously.

I freed myself from Jules' embrace and felt in my pocket for my card.

'Oh!' He whistled softly. 'I see!'

It was clear he'd have given two months' salary for this cursed train to have gone off the rails at Melun.

'Here come the crime squad,' announced the uniformed cop, who'd been leaning out of the window. Some men in felt hats climbed into the carriage.

'Here's yet *another* brown trilby, dirty mac and pair of handlebars!' I laughed. Their owner gave a chuckle that made his grey moustache tilt up at the ends.

'Well, well! If it isn't Nestor Burma!' he cried.

'Hallo, Superintendent Faroux!' I answered, giving my old friend his newly acquired title.

'You're very free with the soft soap today. You . . . ' He let out an oath. He'd just seen the dead body.

'What's this?' he exclaimed. 'A case of split personality?'

A well-read man, Florimond Faroux!

The railway police office at the Gare de Lyon was a frightful hole, like most of its kind. The walls were covered with posters prohibiting this, that and the other in two languages, together with a fly-blown portrait of the head of state. A stove of peace-time dimensions contained a couple of lumps of coal gleaming meagrely through the mica window. M. Belloir, the presiding genius, was rocking to and fro on his shabby chair. When he wasn't staring into space wondering why he hadn't taken a nice peaceful job on the Métro, he was gazing with obvious nausea at a little metal plaque stamped with Gothic lettering and a swastika. M. Belloir had all the facial characteristics, unmistakable to a skilled physiognomist like me, of a dyed-in-the-wool xenophobe. And, as we soon discovered, two years of Occupation hadn't changed his views for the better.

'A Serb!' he groaned for the tenth time. 'Filthy wog!' He pushed a passport across the desk – the passport found on the body. Faroux leafed through it while I looked on.

It concerned one Milan Kostich, born 1903 in Belgrade. The said Kostich had grey eyes, broad features, receding hair and a few other unremarkable peculiarities. His moustache was mentioned and appeared in the photo. With the passport was an identity card issued in 1937 by the Berlin police, and an *Ausweis* for crossing the demarcation line. All this, plus the Hitler emblem also found on the corpse, was very displeasing to Superintendent Belloir, who already couldn't bear foreigners and now found another one standing between him and his pension. Defunct, certainly, but more of a pest that way than if he'd been alive.

Florimond Faroux didn't seem very happy either. He kept chewing at his moustache. By way of variation he would pluck a speck of dust from his trouser leg. Every forty seconds precisely he adjusted the angle of his chocolate-brown hat. Then he pulled himself together.

'We'd better do it by the book,' he announced, with a determination born of despair. 'We'll need someone to take notes. Perhaps your secretary could oblige?'

The secretary lit a cigarette as if it was going to be his last and sat down to his typewriter. Faroux asked me to repeat my story and I was quite willing. The sooner everyone realized I was telling the truth and knew no more than they did about this murder, the sooner they'd set me free to go and have a much-needed drink. So I explained how I'd been on my way back from Marseilles where I'd had to go on business. An industrialist called Robert Beaucher had asked me to recover some passionate love letters from a siren who knew a thing or two about valuable manuscripts. She'd been threatening to send this lot to the lady wife of the aforementioned Beaucher. As usual, the great Nestor Burma had succeeded in his mission.

Faroux didn't ask me to go into detail. He couldn't

have cared less about why I'd gone to Marseilles. He knew I was perfectly capable of making up a highly convincing spiel to account for my journey, anyway. What did interest him – watch it! he was serious now – was this business about moustaches and look-alike clothes.

'It's all very difficult,' he said with a sidelong glance at M. Belloir, who nodded lugubriously. 'If it weren't for that bloody badge . . . By the way, I've never seen one like that before. Have you?'

'No,' I said, 'nor have I.'

'I know the various emblems of the SS and the SA, and any number of other groups in the army and the party, but this one I don't. Have *you* any idea what it might be?'

I said no. It wasn't entirely a lie.

'If it wasn't for that swastika you'd be home by now. But I want to get this business sorted out so as not to be in trouble with the Germans . . . and I don't want them to think I've disregarded any evidence.'

'Naturally not.'

'Besides, I can't just ignore what Madame . . . er . . . Madame' (he flipped through some grubby papers) . . . what Madame Flamant says, simply because you're a detective and she's only a shopkeeper. We can't afford to discriminate against *them* nowadays. And she's very critical of your behaviour. "Strange and suspicious" are the words she used.'

'Mme Flamant? That'll be Jules's wife?'

'Precisely. You were in her company for part of the journey and insulted her on the subject of the Allied landing . . . I didn't gather whether you were for or against.'

'Oh, no! don't *you* start! What I was against was silly

chatter. I told her and her husband and three others to pack it in – it was bad manners to talk about the war.'

'Bad manners, he says!' sighed Faroux. 'Anyhow, after you'd said your piece, you moved to another compartment. And just now, when the train got in, Milan Kostich's body was discovered by some of the passengers, including M. and Mme Flamant. She'd just recognized it as that of the rude man of the previous evening when you spoke to her . . . Question number one: what were you doing in that carriage anyway?'

'Just as I was coming out of the station I met the stationmaster and two cops coming in the other direction looking excited. My professional interest was aroused.'

'Right. Now: why did you have a moustache when you left Marseilles and *not* have one when you reached Paris?'

I explained about the beautiful blonde spy.

'Right,' he said again. He'd known me long enough to be sure that on this subject at least I was telling the the truth. He asked me a few more questions. Had I noticed a man dressed like me on the platform at the Gare St-Charles? Had I met him in the corridor during the journey? I said I hadn't, and the interview came to an end. I signed my statement and accepted Faroux's apologies – I understood, didn't I, that he couldn't ignore Mme Flamant and her misgivings, especially as the Germans were bound to come poking their noses into the case. I grabbed my bags and left.

As I walked by the left-luggage office I passed two types in loden overcoats, leather gloves and green hats. They had red faces and gold-rimmed spectacles. Gestapo.

Good luck to you, Superintendent Belloir, I thought.

3 The death of Nestor Burma

The brass doorknob shone like a new penny. Above the bell-push the name Hélène Chatelain, cut out of a visiting card, was propped lopsidedly in the metal slot. I could hear a voice coming from inside. A cracked, elderly voice: ' . . . our Empire . . . terrible misfortune . . . armistice . . . we shall defend . . . ' It was the radio, broadcasting a message from Pétain about the events in Algeria. I interrupted the harangue with a series of rapid rings at the bell and Hélène came to the door.

'Good morning, boss!' She was just out of bed; it was eleven o'clock.

'When the cat's away the mice will play.'

'Very original,' she mocked. 'You should travel more often, it broadens the mind. But you must admit it's warmer here than at the agency.' She nodded towards the electric fire.

'You have a point there. I suppose I could manage . . . '

'Oh, thank you, darling, thank you!' she simpered. 'So you *do* love your little Hélène!'

'Stop this nonsense and give me a drink – I've got a terrible hangover.'

She produced a not very full bottle of brandy and a large glass. 'This'll do the trick.'

I drank, watched by my secretary, her pretty face lit by a smile.

'I say,' she remarked, 'have you been in a catfight? Or did you shave off your moustache deliberately? You must have hated giving it up!'

'I removed it in the loo on the train, by the light of a blacked-out bulb and using a blunt razor-blade.'

'You poor dear! Thank you!'

'I didn't do it to please you. I did it because I wanted to sleep with a beautiful blonde spy and the moustache was putting her off.'

'A beautiful spy! How exciting! It must've been an eventful trip!'

'Very. When we got to Paris there was a corpse in one of the compartments.'

'That doesn't surprise me. Who was it?'

'A man called Milan Kostich, a Serb. He and I patronize the same men's outfitters.' I described his appearance. Hélène grew serious. Her grey eyes took on a steely glint.

'And you believe . . . '

'Yes. I know it sounds far-fetched, but I can't help thinking Kostich has gone to heaven, hell or purgatory, as the case may be, on a ticket intended for me.'

I poured myself another drink.

'It's going to cause no end of a row,' I said. 'This guy was a member of the Nazi party – perhaps even of some secret section of it – and the Germans'll go mad. The Algerian landing was making them touchy already.'

'Yes, what about the landing? Will it—'

'Stop, stop!' I protested. 'Talk about something else!'

I knocked back my brandy, left half my luggage with Hélène and went off home to think and to sleep. Especially to sleep.

*

There was something to be said for the landing, though. It had let me see through my client's deception. To think I'd fallen for it, and been prepared to spread it around that he was a fat man called Robert Beaucher! It was all lies. Actually he was thin, and his real name was Fred Astaire. And there he was, laughing his head off at the joke he'd played on me, and tap-dancing on the kitchen table with Ginger Rogers. They were making a terrible racket. She was wearing Jackie Lamour's black leotard, with only her face and legs visible. I would have known her by those legs alone, being something of an expert on the subject. But I'd nearly mistaken her for the owner of the costume! It must have been the food rationing – it does affect your judgement. Anyway, now I'd be able to explain everything, but I'd have to wait until they'd finished their number, and it looked as if that might take some time. They *were* making a din!

All of a sudden a disembodied voice bawled above the noise, 'Hell, are you going to open this door or not?'

Everything changed.

Fred Astaire must have said something nasty about me, and now I can't stand the Brits or the Yanks. I've declared war on England and America, and I'm at the battle of Waterloo. We're taking a hiding, but 'The Guards die – they do not surrender!' A beaten-up old 'taxi of the Marne' arrives on the battlefield, and out gets Marshal Pétain, marking time with his walking stick as he goes along, and making even more noise than Fred and Ginger. He pins a badge with Gothic letters and a swastika on it to my chest. Loud applause! Hitler makes a speech and bangs on the furniture.

Someone was knocking on the door, and might have been giving it the odd kick as well.

An oath was all the greeting I got from my two callers as I let them in.

'You're a heavy sleeper!' growled one of them.

'The sleep of the just,' I said.

'Oh yeah? Anyhow, the chief wants to see you.'

'The chief of the crime squad?'

'That's the one – M. Harvet himself. Hurry up and get dressed.'

Their eyes roved around the room, listing the objects they could smash up if they ever got to search it.

Five-thirty by my watch. I went to the window and looked out. It was getting dark and there was a fine slanting drizzle. I picked up my clothes and went into the bathroom. The inspectors followed dutifully.

'I suppose this is about train 108?' I said.

They pretended they didn't know what I was talking about.

Fifteen minutes later I was in an office on the Quai des Orfèvres. Curtains shut out the fading light. The coal shortage didn't seem to be much of a problem here. Behind a paper-strewn desk sat M. Arthur Harvet. Also present was Benoît, a detective from Security, plus someone the first two kept smarmily addressing as 'chief'. He must be the head of the Sûreté. Besides them there was a pretty, fair youth with a military air in spite of his civvy suit, and another man with a vaguely familiar look about him. He smoked a cigar and was red as to face, green as to hat and gold-rimmed as to spectacles. We'd met before.

When I'd sat down, Harvet showed me a file. It was a collection of tittle-tattle about me, piously assembled by his colleagues in the Ministry of the Interior and covering the period from my first communion to my latest row with the landlord. I glanced through it, filling my pipe.

'Well,' I inquired. 'So what?'

' "So what?"!' yelped Benoît of Security. 'We've got an oddball here!'

Harvet made a gesture of impatience and shut the folder.

'We've a favour to ask you,' he announced. 'It's in your own interests and the interests of justice not to refuse. We've got special reasons for not revealing the identity of the man who was murdered on train 108, and for wanting it to be thought the victim was someone else. It so happens that you're his double, or near enough. We hope we can rely on your . . . er . . . cooperation.' His eyes strayed to my file.

'We want you to retire to the country for a bit and let people believe you're dead.'

He gave an embarrassed smile. He reminded me of the railway Superintendent. Had the Serbian stiff any idea how much trouble he was causing the French top brass?

'We'll arrange a funeral worthy of a great detective. Do you accept our proposal?'

Him and his 'we'!

'Have I got any choice?'

He shrugged. 'There are worse things than being temporarily out of circulation.'

'As it happens, I was thinking of taking a holiday.'

'Good! Where were you thinking of going?'

'Some of the hotels in Fontainebleau have got heating.'

'The Black Eagle, for example.'

'The Black Eagle it is, then. But . . . er . . . there might be problems . . . ' I rubbed my forefinger and thumb together meaningly.

'Money? That'll be taken care of.'

'Fine then.' I was getting up to go but he motioned me

to wait. The fair youth began speaking in German to the man with the green hat, who listened in silence, nodding from time to time. When the translation of the interview was finished, he trained his cold pale gaze on me.

'You will not regret it,' he brought out slowly.

I did my good citizen act. 'It's my duty to do all in my power to further the cause of law and order,' I declared, laughing up my sleeve.

'*Dank.*'

The chief of the Sûreté, who until then had kept mum, now piped up.

'A car will collect you first thing tomorrow morning and take you to Fontainebleau.'

I thanked them for their kindness and left. In the corridor outside I bumped into Faroux. He'd dearly have loved to avoid me, but he couldn't.

'I hope you're not afraid of ghosts,' I joked. 'You see before you a dead man!'

He looked anxiously round the empty passage. 'Don't be an idiot!' he whispered. 'Give the legend of Dynamite Burma a rest for a while and keep quiet. Or you might really end up inside the empty coffin they'll be carrying out of your place tomorrow morning.'

As I was thinking things over at home, I began to have misgivings. At that moment the telephone rang. When I answered, the caller hung up.

'Well, well!' I thought. 'They're checking to see I haven't skipped.' I filled my pipe. When the phone rang again I snatched it up. 'Hallo?' They hung up once more. 'Good old Florimond!' I thought.

It was 11.30 by my watch. I put my stock of the soothing weed in my pocket, cast an eye round to make sure there wasn't anything incriminating lying about, put on my hat and trenchcoat and pushed off. The telephone went again at one point, but I let it ring.

It was filthy weather out. The street was wet, cold and deserted. No suspicious shadowy figures to be seen. But hearing a car approach I concealed myself in a doorway. The car drove past, spraying muddy water as it went, and stopped in front of my flat. Several men got out. Boots clomped on the pavement. Electric torches flashed – the beam from one of them glinted on the barrel of a sub-machine gun.

I could still hear my nocturnal visitors from the next street, hammering on the door and cursing the concierge.

4 The plots thicken

It was a night of surprises. Faroux got his share when he reached home well after midnight, and coming round the last turn in the stairs found me sitting peacefully on the doormat.

'Well, I'm damned!' he gasped. 'You've got a nerve!'

'Ssh!' I said. 'Everyone's asleep. Police Superintendents aren't supposed to disturb the peace.'

He wouldn't be a Superintendent for long, he grumbled, if he went on associating with me. He finally managed to find the keyhole and I followed him into the flat. He plugged in an electric fire and I sat down. My wet garments began to steam. Faroux moved about the room, not speaking.

'Don't pull a face like that,' I said. 'After your silent phone calls where did you expect me to go? I came here because nobody would suspect I'd hide in a copper's place. And also because you're the only one who can give me some information. I take it that on reflection old Rote-Kartoffel changed his mind about the scheme for having me go and play dead all on my own in the sticks . . . '

'Who's Rote-Kartoffel?'

'The Pink Potato – that's what I call the man with the

green hat. Who is he? A member of the German police, I suppose?'

'Yes. His name's Otto Schirach.'

'I presume he had second thoughts and decided I'd be less tempted to step out of line in a cell at the Santé or Fresnes. You found out, and . . . Still, I must say you left your warning till pretty late . . . And now . . . ' (I paused to light my pipe) 'kindly tell me what can of worms I've somehow managed to open.'

'All right. Listen. The French police are supposed to have been taken off this case, but I consider it my duty to go on taking an interest in it . . . unofficially.' He gave me a conspiratorial look, signifying 'Need I say more?'

'So I've been collecting as much information as I can. In the first place, the dead man wasn't called Kostich: his real name was Sdenko Matich . . . '

'Not much of an improvement.'

' . . . and he was a Croat.'

'Hard luck on your pal at the Gare de Lyon! He had difficulty swallowing a Serb – a Croat will finish him off!'

Faroux shrugged impatiently. 'Also – and this is what's upsetting the Germans – Matich used to be an agent in a branch of the Nazi secret service, one stage higher than the Gestapo. A kind of secret service personal to Hitler.'

'I'd guessed something of the sort,' I told him. 'The badge found on the body was issued by that organization, I suppose?'

'Yes. But Matich was no longer a member. There was some kind of funny business a few years back. He was an expert on oil . . . '

'That's bad! Very inflammable! Was he blown?'

'I get the impression he left of his own accord. And after that the Gestapo or some such were after him to have a chat.'

'But it wasn't the Gestapo that rubbed him out?'

'No, that's the funny part of it. Instead of being glad someone else had got rid of their quitter for them, the Germans appear to be miffed.'

'Professional pride,' I suggested. 'They'd rather have done the job themselves.'

'Maybe. In any case, what they'd like now is to find out who did it and why. And they're letting the murderer think he killed the wrong man to see if it'll make him give himself away. The death of Nestor Burma is going to be splashed all over the papers. I've just been to the office of the *Matin*. They're giving you a two-column obituary. And it really goes to town!'

'Wait till you see our friend Marc Covet's effort in the *Crépuscule*! That'll put the *Matin*'s in the shade. Just think of all the bitchy remarks he'll be able to make! Still,' I added, serious again, 'surely that won't fool the murderer – he must know who it was he killed!'

'Of course,' conceded Faroux. 'Especially as he went off with the victim's effects.'

'His luggage was taken, was it?'

'Unless he was travelling without any . . . Anyway, Otto Schirach and co. don't seem to be bothering with details like that. They're relying on their wheeze of changing the identity of the victim to trick the murderer into making a blunder.'

'I'd have expected better of the German genius,' I sighed. 'Another illusion down the drain. They won't be too pleased to have me on the loose, will they?'

'They certainly won't. I advise you to be careful.'

'That's why I came here. Though perhaps I should

have gone to Hélène's – she's prettier than you, and she usually gives me a drink. By the way, do you suppose she could be in trouble as the runaway detective's secretary? I wouldn't want that.'

'I don't imagine so. We didn't give them any details about your agency.'

'Gosh, if the Occupation goes on for another ten years the cops'll become quite popular!'

'But I still don't think it'd be wise for you to see Mlle Chatelain,' he went on, ignoring my sarcasm. 'And if you have a bank, don't go there either. Places like that are usually watched.'

'I shan't need to go near either Hélène or the bank. My client in Marseilles supplied me with enough of the ready to last several weeks.'

'That's good!' he said a bit too promptly. He was relieved not to have to fork out for a loan.

'Let's get back to Sdenko Matich,' I said. 'What was the cause of death?'

'He stopped three 7.65s full in the chest. He was in a sitting position. There was no struggle. He must have been facing the murderer, and it must have been someone he knew.'

'Is that so?'

'Does it surprise you?'

'No. Carry on.'

'The passengers in the compartments on either side didn't hear any shots.'

'Using a silencer, was he?'

'Probably. The murder was committed during the night. I don't recall the exact time the forensic expert gave, but it happened after the train crossed the demarcation line.'

'Of course. Otherwise it wouldn't have been discovered

in Paris. Is there any information on the Croat's fellow passengers?'

'Not a thing. The murderer must have moved to another coach as soon as the deed was done, and nipped off the train when he reached his destination.'

'Do you think he got off in Paris?'

'We don't know. That's the Germans' problem.'

'But the French police are following the case?'

'Very much so. We'd like to know why the occupying forces are so interested in a chap they should be glad to see the back of. And as Matich was travelling from Marseilles I'm going to take a trip down there.'

'I wouldn't mind going back to the Unoccupied Zone for a bit, either,' said I. 'Up here they're out to give me a hard time, and hiding out somewhere twiddling my thumbs is not my style. Only there's the line to cross, and my name must be familiar now to the border control. I'll need false papers. And you're in a better position than anyone to get me some.

'Listen,' I added persuasively, 'with an assistant of my calibre, the solution to the mystery's in the bag. You know me.' (His eyes said 'Yes, unfortunately', though he bit back the words.) 'But if you like I'll give you further proof of my abilities. Remember the badge found on the body? I'd never seen it before, but I knew right away it was the emblem of some sort of secret service. When he went through the demarcation line Matich boasted to the border control officer that he was in the Nazi police.'

'How do *you* know?' barked Faroux, now extremely suspicious.

'The fact that he and I looked alike – at that point I still had my moustache – and were dressed alike, made the German officer say a very funny thing: *Diese Polizisten sind alle Brüder*. Do you know German?'

'Good God, no!' he spluttered angrily. Comical chap.

'It means "These policemen are all brothers". At the time I didn't understand, but this morning, at the station, everything became clear.'

Faroux frowned. 'Hm,' he growled, unconvinced. 'That's one explanation, I suppose . . . Look here, Burma . . . ' And he started trying to tell me I was wrong to suspect him of fraternizing. I said my asking if he spoke German wasn't meant to be offensive. But he still went rambling on, obviously sorry he'd ever brought the matter up.

At 5 a.m., when the curfew ended, I left. By then a lot of ideas had occurred to me about Sdenko Matich. But as Florimond was being so unhelpful I wasn't going to share them with *him*.

The morning mist was icy, and I was glad to dive into the Métro as soon as the trains started running. Down there in the warm I read through most of the dailies. Roosevelt and I shared the limelight. I had the advantage – no one was calling *me* a treacherous swine. It was the famous detective this, the famous detective that – the people who were after me were certainly doing things in style. Every paper had a photo of me with a great moustache, added on by the Gestapo retouchers, that made me look even more like Sdenko Matich than I really was.

FAMOUS PRIVATE EYE STRUCK DOWN BY ASSASSIN
NESTOR BURMA SLAIN
Death of 'tec who could K.O. any mystery,

lamented the compliant scribes. This terrible tragedy was the work of gangsters – of the Gaullists – of British agents – of the Vichy cabal. You could take your pick.

When I'd finished chuckling, I went and called on a

film make-up man, a Russian I'd met once when I was working as an extra. Boris hadn't seen the papers yet, so I broke the news that I was dead. By this time I *was* half dead with fatigue. He was thrilled when I asked him to do a bit of work on my face. He asked me numerous questions which I didn't answer, and did a grand job on me without using any false hair. The last thing I needed was to look like the press photos. In exchange for his trouble and as an inducement to silence I gave him a thousand-franc note. It was in two pieces joined together with sticky tape, and he examined it closely in case the numbers in the different halves didn't match. In his outlandish French he told me how careful you had to be when notes had been cut up like that. And started to tell me the old story about the banknote made up of tiny strips from a hundred, two hundred, a thousand others – the number varies in each version.

When I'd left him it occurred to me this case was definitely beginning to look like the League of Nations. A Croat, some Germans, a Russian – I could do with a Pole. Marc Covet drank enough to qualify. I went off to pay him a visit.

He'd just heard on the radio about my death, and he downed a good half-bottle of wine to help him get over the shock. This was the first time he'd had a social call from a ghost. But any excuse would do for a bender.

'There's one good thing about the Occupation,' I told him, setting down my glass. 'Journalists like you, who aren't fully paid-up collaborators, are only allowed to write about people losing their false teeth, or the influence of the trade winds on fashion. So there's no danger of you producing great screeds on the subject when I talk to you about things I'd have taken good care not to mention before the war.'

'What was that all in aid of, my fine phantom friend?' asked Covet, his eyes getting more and more glazed.

'It was in aid of precisely that – my death. Do you know why it occurred? Why a coffin supposedly containing my remains will leave the mortuary this very morning? Why tonight you'll be putting your name to an obituary that you'll find, complete down to the last comma, on the desk in your office?'

'I haven't a clue!'

'Right. Then listen. But remember, you won't be able to use the story.'

And I put him in the picture.

'Pay attention now,' I continued. 'Your taking me in makes you to some extent an accessory after the fact. I'd like your opinion on some ideas of mine I've not let on about to Faroux. First a few words about my recent activities. I'm just back from Marseilles, like Sdenko Matich, only in better condition. I went at the request of a certain Robert Beaucher. An industrialist, a fat chap with a wife and a family I haven't met. He strikes me as a nutter. What he wanted me to do was this: there's a night-club dancer, called Jackie Lamour . . . you don't know her, by any chance?'

'No such luck!'

'Don't worry! She's a menace! Well, she was teaching our industrialist to dance, too – to her tune, at her price. He'd been her lover, of course, and long after he'd ceased to enjoy her favours he was still having to pay up. He'd written her seventeen letters blazing with passion, as they say, and he reckoned they were compromising. And so, judging by the use she was putting them to, did she. Personally, when I read them, I thought they were plain ridiculous. However, he was ready to pay to get them back, and I was the one he asked to do it. She lives in a villa on the outskirts of Marseilles, near Cap Croisette, alone except for a manservant by the name of Joseph. That's where the letters were. Beaucher knew near enough the place she'd hidden them in, and could easily have taken them himself without going to the expense of hiring a detective. But as I said, he's a nutter. He told me the funniest part of the trick would be listening to his tormentor's threats once he'd got the letters back, knowing all the time she was powerless. It would be several days before she noticed they'd disappeared, and as, in spite of everything, they were seeing each other all the time, he intended to have a whale of a spree for those few days, until she found out. And he thought thirty thousand francs was dirt cheap for a pick-me-up like that.'

'Thirty thousand francs? Gosh!'

'As you say. He told me where the house was, the times when I could be sure of not interrupting anything, and the most likely places to look in, and he had a set of duplicate keys made for me. I must say it's the only job I've ever had where that's happened. But I hadn't come all the way from Paris to turn down a lucrative proposition just because the client was up the pole. I agreed to his plan and almost carried it out – but there was a snag.' I told Covet about the clash of arms in Jackie's bedroom, and all that followed after.

'I don't quite see why you're telling me all this,' he said. 'I've been in tighter corners than that, and in your company, what's more. What's the connection between Robert Beaucher and the murdered Croat?'

'To tell you the truth I don't know. But one or two details strike me as interesting.'

'Such as?'

'Well, at first I thought it might be a case of mistaken identity, and that the bullets that sent Sdenko Matich to the great safe house in the sky were intended for me. My theory was that Robert Beaucher, upset because I'd read his maunderings, had sent some thug to get me. But wouldn't that be attaching too much importance both to my client's unbalanced state and to the letters themselves? Apart from their silliness, they contain nothing out of the way. Except for one detail. It's to do with the Croat. Do you remember the name of another Croat, the terrorist who shot Alexander Karageorgevich?'

'Kalemen.'

'And his first name?'

'His first name . . . er . . . now let me see . . . ' Covet poured himself a drink. The effect was instantaneous. 'Petrus.'

'Petrus, eh? Well, this may not mean anything, but the famous letters are signed *Petr*. At the time I read it as Peter, but I remember now: it was definitely *Petr*. Now let's do a recap. In 1934 the Croat *Petrus* Kalemen makes an attempt in *Marseilles* on the life of his beloved king. In 1942 the Croat *Sdenko* Matich, whose double I might be when I have a moustache, is murdered just when I've been to Marseilles and recovered some letters signed *Petr*. On top of that, the person who's been holding the letters is a dubious character with the scar of an old bullet wound on her arm. She didn't cop that in the war or doing the Lambeth Walk. It makes you think.'

'And how!' cried Covet excitedly.

He could already see himself writing the truth, the whole truth and nothing but the truth about the Marseilles Royal Shooting Mystery.

'And the letters themselves?' he demanded suddenly. 'Isn't there anything suspicious in them?'

'Not as far as I could see. All lovey-dovey stuff, sheer garbage. Writing like that to Jackie Lamour is proof of a disturbed mind. She must have fallen about laughing.'

'It might be useful to take another look at them,' Marc suggested. He'd learned from me to leave nothing to chance.

'A bit difficult at the moment,' I pointed out.

There followed not exactly a silence, because wine makes a noise going down the gullet, but a momentary break in the flow of words.

'What do you plan to do?' inquired my friend when our glasses were empty.

'Stop racking my brains and go and ask Beaucher some sharp questions. It may work or it may not. But it'll be better than sitting here theorizing. In any case, I was already intending to go down to the Unoccupied Zone. The Germans will be after me all the time if I stay here.'

'Unoccupied Zone?' sniggered Covet. 'You think the distinction's still valid? Can you see Hitler letting his enemies run around enjoying themselves four hundred kilometres away on the other side of the line, while he stays on this side doing nothing about it? If you think you can get away from the Germans by hopping down to the Midi, you must be barmy yourself. At the office everyone's expecting to hear at any moment that the Wehrmacht has crossed the demarcation line. Take a dekko at that!' He produced a brand new *Ausweis*. 'They're ready printed for us to go and see the German troops parading along the Canebière.'

'I fully realize,' said I, 'that it won't be long before they go and paddle their little boots in the Mediterranean.

But why should that stop me? When the whole country's occupied it'll still be no more dangerous for me down there than up here. And down there I may be able to find out whether the bloke who shot Sdenko Matich got the wrong target. If Robert Beaucher did send some dim hoodlum after *me*, there's going to be fireworks, I can tell you!'

'I hope I'm there to see it!'

'But of course you'll be there! From now on, Marc, you and I are going to do everything together! When you've got me a press pass I'll be one of your fraternity and . . . '

I've never seen anyone put up such a struggle. He even forgot his drink. False papers? False papers? Oh no! Absolutely out of the question, quite imposs . . . Unless . . . perhaps . . . He tossed down a quick one: my hopes revived . . . Why did I need want false papers? I could get across without. Frédéric Delan was our man!

Fred Delan was a psychiatrist to whom I'd once been of assistance and who'd subsequently helped me on some of my cases. A very obliging chap. I'd lost contact with him since just before the war, but it appeared he and Covet were still in touch.

'He owns a private mental home,' he explained, 'at Ferdières, in Saône-et-Loire, down near the demarcation line. Some of the inmates, including Delan himself probably, are real nutcases, and others are not. They're people wanting to escape into the Unoccupied Zone. Delan runs an organization for smuggling people through. I think that's where most of his money comes from.'

'Just the chap I need,' said I.

Covet heaved a sigh of relief.

'I think I can still travel by train without attracting attention,' I went on. 'As long as I don't come across a certain kind of German, I should be all right. I'll go down as soon as possible to this dump you mentioned – Ferdières. Only, since I haven't got a travel permit and I don't fancy queuing at the station for one and then maybe coming away without, I'm going to call on your services again. Newspapers are allotted a few seats on all the trains, aren't they? Get one for me, will you?'

'Yes, I can manage that,' he agreed.

'Marvellous. In the meantime, I'm going to stay here. And will you please try to get in touch with Hélène and tell her I'm all right?'

'OK.' said Marc. The Allied landing was having an effect on him, too. He'd soon have an English accent if he didn't watch out.

5 Asylum nights

It was 3.30 by the station clock when the decrepit old train set me down at Ferdières. There was a nip in the air but the weather was fine.

Marc Covet had given me full instructions so that I could find Fred Delan's clinic without having to ask. I didn't linger in the town, but pipe in mouth, hands in the pockets of my raincoat – for of course I hadn't bothered with luggage – I set off with a casual air towards the country.

The clinic stood on its own outside the town, about a kilometre from the last of the houses. It lay back some distance off the main road, at the end of a rutted driveway. It was built on four floors, and although the stonework of the façade could have done with a good clean the general effect was imposing. Above high surrounding walls you could see the leafless tops of the trees in the extensive grounds.

The entrance was guarded by a grim-looking gate, its bars backed with metal sheeting to thwart curious eyes. A bell-pull was set into the right-hand gate-post and beside it a black marble plaque announced: PSYCHIATRIC CLINIC – DR FREDERIC DELAN. The gold paint had worn off some of the letters.

I pulled the bell, setting off a terrific clanging. At once someone came hurrying to the door. He had a round cap perched on his head, a dirty apron tied round his middle and the unlovely features of a pugilist barred from every ring for hitting below the belt. He had to be the one in charge of violent patients, if there was such a category in this dump. Which I doubted, considering the impressive silence that reigned everywhere. I told him my name was Martin, and that I wished to see the doctor. He should be expecting me, I said, unless there'd been a hold-up in the post. (After my conversation with Covet, I'd written to the doctor under the name of Martin, a pseudonym he knew I used from time to time.)

The bruiser showed me into the waiting-room and then went to 'ask', returning soon afterwards to lead me to an office lined with books and pictures where Frédéric Delan sat in an armchair, waiting. On seeing me he blinked, hesitated briefly, then held out his hand. I shook it warmly.

At that moment in came a blonde cutie in a white overall, a pleasant change from the boxer, who'd made himself scarce. In addition to her considerable natural advantages, she had a tray on which stood a bottle of three-star and two king-size glasses. I deduced that my assumed name still meant something to the doctor. An excellent start.

While Delan poured the drinks I studied him. Apart from having lost some more hair, which made him look very distinguished, he hadn't changed much since we'd last met. His features were still arranged in their usual slightly barmy grin, but that was quite appropriate on a psychiatrist.

'Well!' he said, handing me a glass. 'Your face seems

to have undergone some alterations. I didn't know you at first.'

'So I noticed. You can't imagine how pleased I was. Your hesitation was a compliment to my make-up man. Do I really look different?'

'Yes, very. Anyway,' he chuckled, 'you're not anything like your press photos.'

'Oh, you know about those?'

'Yes. I'd just read about your death in the Paris papers when I got your note. Always up to something, aren't you?'

'That's Nestor Burma for you,' I said modestly.

'Peculiar chap, eh?'

'Someone made much the same remark a few days ago at the Quai des Orfèvres.'

'No! Tell me about it.'

I yawned. 'It's a long story. I'm dead beat, and to tell you the truth I'm still completely at sea. If it's all the same to you I'd rather discuss it later, when I know more of the facts.'

'I see,' he said, nodding sagaciously. 'You don't want to talk about it.'

'There's no keeping secrets from you, doc,' I laughed. 'Yes, between you and me, I'd rather keep mum.'

'Right,' he said peaceably. 'I quite understand. Apart from that, what can I do for you?'

'They're very fond of ghosts on the other side of the line. As a recent corpse, I want to go over there and haunt someone.'

'It's urgent, I suppose?'

'Have you ever know me hang about?'

'Good heavens, no! But there are limits, even if you are Dynamite Burma. Since the landing in North Africa they've tightened up the watch on the line. Normally there should have been some people crossing tomorrow, but the man taking them over tells me we'll need to wait a bit. The lads are working out a new route. I've got three clients here as anxious as you are to get to the Unoccupied Zone. They're waiting. You'll have to do the same and not start breaking up the furniture to make your point. Otherwise,' he joked, 'I'll be forced to keep you on as a patient!'

'I'll be as quiet as a lamb,' I promised. 'How long do you think it'll be?'

'I can't tell. An opportunity could crop up and then the guides would rush here in the middle of the night to pick up their group. It's happened before. Or it could be several days. More brandy?'

'Yes, please.' I shrugged resignedly. I couldn't risk crossing by myself. 'So what happens now?'

'You said you needed a rest. I'll arrange a room for you.'

'With padded walls?'

He laughed. 'Of course. A hyperactive subject like you . . . '

'Tell me – how much will the crossing cost me?'

'Be my guest. Just give the guide a good tip. Yes, yes, I insist. But when you've dealt with the person you're going to get even with, come and tell me all about it.'

'Done.'

I rose. Delan pressed a button and in came the comely blonde.

'Jeanne, this is M. Martin – a new patient. Take him to room 6, please. He's an alcoholic.'

The girl cast an ironical glance from her employer to me, taking in the bottle on the way. 'I thought as much,' she observed.

'And with you in the room, baby,' I said, 'I can feel sex mania coming on too.'

It wasn't a padded cell, but the window was heavily barred. The room was on the second floor, at the front of the building overlooking the drive. Through a thin line of trees I could see the main road. Night was falling and the landscape was tinged with purple. Suddenly a flock of rooks rose cawing from a copse.

It wasn't a very cheerful scene and I closed the window with a sinking feeling. Pulling myself together I filled my pipe, turned on the feeble light and closed the black-out curtains, as instructed by a notice on the door. In my bathroom I found everything I needed for a shave and wash and brush up, after which I went downstairs to see Delan.

'I thought you were exhausted,' he said.

'Not now I know you're not going to bombard me with questions.'

'We'll talk about the weather then, shall we?'

'If you don't mind.'

'All right, we'll do it over dinner – it'll soon be time. We'll eat in my private quarters. It's better you shouldn't mix with what you might call my transient clients.'

This arrangement suited me, and I did justice to a meal such as I'd not enjoyed for many a long day. We were waited on by Jeanne who, out of consideration for my alcoholism, always left the wine bottle where I could reach it for myself.

When the table had been cleared I sat back with a contented sigh and took out my pipe. My host lit a cigar.

'You do have real loonies here too, don't you?' I asked.

'Yes. I'd have to, anyway, as camouflage. They're not

really mad, though. Just depressives who've come here
for treatment, not at all your textbook cases of dementia,
shouting and cursing and throwing their food about.
They're very quiet and well behaved. And they live
more or less as members of the household, in the rear
part of the building.'

'So they're not likely to keep me awake at night?'

'Not at all. Though . . . Look here, Burma, I may
as well tell you this straight away so as not to have you
grousing at me later on. There's only one incurable case
here, and he has the room next to yours. I've never let
him mix with the other patients in case he upsets them.
He sometimes has attacks in the form of nightmares, and
then he shouts a bit. These fits of rage – no, that's too
strong a word, excitement is more like it – they never last
long. He's a friend of mine, and I've tried everything to
cure him, but it's no use. His name's Victor Fernèse –
you may have heard of him.'

'No,' I replied. 'You and I may have worked together,
but I don't know all your friends.'

'It isn't just as my friend you might have heard of
him. Didn't you belong to various pacifist organizations
before the war?'

'Yes.'

'Fernèse too. He was a militant. I thought perhaps
at some of the meetings . . . '

I racked my brain but no, the name Victor Fernèse
didn't ring any bells.

'Perhaps he was using another name,' suggested Delan.
'Anyway, he was a pacifist who lived for his ideals. He
dreaded the storm that was about to break over us. When
war was declared in 1939 all his illusions crumbled, the
shock sent him out of his mind overnight. I heard about
it in a letter from someone I know in Toulouse – he'd

been working near there, at Saint-Gaudens. I had Fernèse
brought here as a patient. I couldn't be called up – there's
something wrong with one of my lungs – so I went on
treating him as best I could but, as I told you, without
success. I've given up hope of a cure now, but I keep
him on. I'm hiding him really. The Germans aren't keen
on pacifists like Fernèse – they know who their enemies
are – and I'd rather have my friend here with me than in
their hands.'

'And is he still subject to attacks?'

'Brief ones, yes. He goes into a dream and stays like
that for hours, muttering. Then he livens up and calls
out the name of a woman, Laurence. I didn't know he'd
ever been involved with anyone of that name.'

'You can't be expected to know everything.'

'Not even how to cure a friend's illness, for all my
qualifications.'

'Come, come, doc. Don't talk so soppy – it doesn't
suit you. When you have a real friend to stay you put
him next door to a noisy nutter.'

'Fernèse can go for weeks without opening his lips.'

'Maybe, but it'd be just my luck if he opened them
tonight.'

'Good grief, Burma, have another drink and stop
moaning. And if your next-door neighbour does have
an attack, don't go banging on the wall to make him
keep quiet – you'll only make him worse. Wait for it to
pass naturally.'

I obeyed his instruction about the drink, but had
another moan as I stood up to go.

The central heating was on in my room and it was
pleasantly warm. I got between the sheets and turned
off the light.

Although, despite my predictions, my mad neighbour

didn't disturb me, I didn't sleep well. I'd barely been in bed for ten minutes and was starting to drop off when I heard the drone of engines. I told myself it must be English planes. The local scenery was about to undergo some modifications, and if my luck was out I was very likely to get a biff on the boko myself. But the planes went over and nothing happened. They were flying low and making a terrible racket. They were too low, in fact, and too noisy to be English planes. This was reassuring in a way but no good as a lullaby.

There were a few seconds of silence and then all hell broke loose out on the road. Backfirings, rumblings – it was as if an earthquake were shaking the clinic to its foundations. The windows went on rattling for ages.

I got out of bed, drew back the curtains without switching on the light, and opened the window. It was a clear night. Peering between the bars I could see the road beyond the leafless trees. It was swarming with large cars scorching along, the light from their dimmed headlamps scarcely touching the ground. They were followed by heavy lorries, then by artillery and tanks of all sizes.

Marc Covet must have used his new *Ausweis*. For this was it: the Axis forces were crossing the line.

'It was only to be expected,' said Delan next morning when I went to his office.

I looked out into the grounds. Three figures were moving about in the pale sunshine. 'For me it's a nuisance,' I said. 'It'll interfere with my crossing, won't it?'

'Yes.' He joined me at the window. 'Look, there's Fernèse going for his walk with Pierre – that's the male nurse.'

I ran my eye over the sick man out there with the bruiser I'd seen the previous day. But I couldn't really be bothered with Victor Fernèse. My mind was full of this new invasion that was going to keep me stuck here for goodness knows how many weeks. I had a look at him just the same. He was a small man of between forty and fifty, with grey hair showing under a dark skullcap. He looked as if his physical health was all right. I'd never seen him before.

I left the doctor to his work and went up to my room, where I spent the rest of the day reading and smoking, assisted in this latter occupation by Bodyguard Pierre. Pierre Pradel to give him his full name. The ex-boxer improved on acquaintance: for something like the price of a pre-war bicycle he let me have some 'home-grown' tobacco which, mixed with Belgian and shag, was not entirely unworthy of my old pipe.

Three days passed in this way, without incident.

On the evening of the fourth day, when we were dining together as usual, Delan gave me some news.

'I don't think it'll be long before you're leaving us. One can never be sure, of course, but I've just had a visit from one of the guides. He advises extreme caution. You'll need to keep clear of the usual crossing-places – they're crawling with grey uniforms. But round about Saint-Alter – he showed me a dot on the map a long way from Ferdières – 'there's still a possibility. The experts have been looking into it today. If all's gone well they'll be here at dawn tomorrow to collect you and the others. You'll spend the day in a farmhouse at Saint-Alter, and go over the line as soon as it gets dark.'

'Perfect!'

We exchanged a few words about Adolf Hitler, as

millions of other people all over the world must have been doing at that moment, and then, while he went off for a game of bridge with three others bound like me for the Unoccupied Zone, I went up to bed.

It was still very early. The house was full of familiar domestic noises. I heard bodyguard Pierre come in next door for a chat with Victor Fernèse, and wondered whether it was good for the patient. Pierre's was the sort of face that can bring on premature births. Passing my door as he went away he called out goodnight. Later I heard the footsteps of the fair Jeanne creeping past, then the sound of doors closing, and the house fell silent, while a sharp November wind howled spitefully outside.

I knew it. It was a very bad idea for bodyguard Pierre, with his face like a busted boot, to go making night-time calls on a nutcase. And sure enough, I was still awake when suddenly I heard cries coming from Fernèse's room next door. He must be having an attack. Up till today he'd kept quiet, waiting for what I hoped was my last night here to make himself heard. And was he letting rip! At first I couldn't grasp what he was yelling about, but after a bit I made out the woman's name the medic had mentioned.

'Laurence! Laurence!' It was Laurence he wanted all right, but he wasn't asking very nicely. It sounded as if he was furious with her, and a bit frightened too. The doxy must have led him a dog's life. He uttered her name again several times in a piercing scream: 'Laurence! Laurence!' Then he burst out laughing. 'Formula 5 . . . Formula 5 . . . ' He gave another dreadful laugh and fell silent.

I found myself heaving a sigh of relief. The Grand

Guignol performance hadn't lasted more than a few seconds, but it wasn't conducive to sleep.

My neighbour's attack seemed not to have disturbed the rest of the household and silence now reigned once more. In this peculiar clinic the temporary inmates took little interest in one another. Discretion was in everybody's interest. And after all there was nothing unexpected about the presence of a madman in what purported to be a madhouse.

As a matter of fact Fernèse, with his intermittent attacks, must provide Delan with excellent cover, justifying the existence of the clinic and masking its function as a staging post. I wondered whether the doctor had really wanted his patient to be cured.

I started to think about the form of the unfortunate chap's mania. Perhaps it *was* the war that had sent him round the bend – I could remember being pretty upset myself in September 1939. But there must be something else in his case. The shouting about Laurence and Formula 5 suggested that Cupid must have given him a good knock on the head with a quiverful of arrows. Formula 5 must be some tricky bit out of the Kama Sutra which Laurence had refused to go along with, and this was what had sent Fernèse round the twist. But I was no Charcot or Freud, and I couldn't go rooting around in the murky corners of people's souls. This bloke would just have to manage as best he could with his Laurence and his Formula 5 and his pal Delan. I'd better watch out if I didn't want to finish up like him. After all, I already had this compulsion to look at pretty girls' legs . . . Then a middle-aged man asked me for a light and it dawned on me that I was asleep and dreaming.

*

The bloke who woke me up some hours later wasn't after a light for a fag – more like a chance to extinguish me for good. Vaguely, in my sleep, I'd heard some sort of commotion in the house, and thought it was the mad chap starting up again. Then the noises became more distinct: people running along the passages, doors being slammed, someone shouting. I got out of bed but I didn't have all my wits about me, perhaps because of all the red wine I'd drunk at dinner. However I soon got them back – though not for long – when I saw my unexpected visitor opening the door and sliding his massive bulk into the room. Before I could make a move or utter a word he'd switched on the meagre light and I could see the steely blue glint of a Mauser aimed at my navel.

'Quiet now, pal,' hissed the intruder. 'This isn't going to hurt – much!' And he gave me a sensational crack with either his fist or the butt of his gun, I don't know which. I sank to the floor, while he withdrew, double-locking the door behind him after considerately turning off the light.

I lay where I was for a while, wondering whether I was adrift in a boat and in the throes of seasickness. Or perhaps I was a German military target just before the start of an air raid, or a parachutist in free fall after a copious meal. My head seemed to have swelled to an enormous size and the room was going round and round. As, aching and confused, I at last staggered to my feet, I heard someone being hauled along the corridor outside, shouting 'Laurence! Laurence' as he went.

This was followed by muttered oaths and a furious female voice saying 'Don't you start your silly nonsense again!' She used a choicer word, actually.

Fernèse started to shout 'Laur . . . ' once more, but the sound died in his throat. They must have gagged

him. Then it sounded as if an army was rushing down
the stairs, and I noticed the distant noise of an engine
running. I could hear people leaving the building and
muttering outside. Quietly I opened the window. In the
cold moonlight a sleek, dark-coloured car stood outside
the gate, its bonnet pointing towards the main road. Two
men, one of them my attacker, went through the gate
and towards the car, humping a struggling but silent
white bundle – Fernèse, I assumed, in his nightclothes
and gagged. They were followed by a woman. She went
round the car and climbed in on the other side, but was
soon summoned to lend the others a hand. As she got out
of the car again I caught a glimpse of a long silk-clad leg.
Then the rest of her appeared. I could see her as clear
as daylight as she helped her accomplices to stow their
victim into the back seat. I wasn't taken completely by
surprise, because the sight of the silken leg had started
my mind working. But it was a bit of a shock just the
same. The kidnapper of mad Victor Fernèse was none
other than lovely Jackie Lamour.

After a few seconds I regained all the faculties that have
earned me my fame and my nickname. The lower part of
my face still didn't feel too good, but the grey cells were
starting to function again. Putting on my trousers and
shoes I went into the bathroom and fetched a sturdily
made stool to smash the lock on the door. People were
beginning to stir in the other rooms. Here and there I
could hear them banging on their doors, locked as mine
had been by Jackie Lamour's friends.

'All clear!' I called. 'Go back to bed, and to sleep if you
can. The director will explain everything in the morning.'
This little speech had a fairly soothing effect, and I went
off downstairs to Fred Delan's private quarters. The door

stood wide open. I rushed to the bedroom: his bed hadn't been slept in. I ran towards the office. As I passed the foot of the stairs I heard someone coming down. It was Jeanne, in bedroom slippers and a somewhat tatty dressing-gown, her blonde hair untidy and her face shiny with overnight cream.

'Hi, baby!' I said. 'Did you know the loonies from a rival establishment had been to serenade us?'

'What?' she stammered.

'Didn't you have a visit from a gentleman with a gun?'

'Do you think you could be a bit clearer . . . ?'

'Later. At the moment I'm looking for the doctor. He's not in his bedroom.'

'He was working tonight . . . he should be in his office.'

'Let's go together. I don't like the look of this – he ought to be going round reassuring his patients.'

The door of the director's office was open and the room was in darkness. I switched on the light. My misgivings were justified: the psychiatrist lay on the carpet, his head and shoulders in a pool of blood.

'I hope the poor chap's not dead!' I exclaimed. 'That would be very inconvenient.'

Bending down, I saw that his eyes were blank and fixed. Swearing, I tried to raise him to a sitting position, but this kind of first aid has never been known to work with anyone as dead as he was. I allowed the corpse to sink back on the floor. 'Bloody hell!' I groaned. I was extremely annoyed.

It wasn't much of a funeral oration, but luckily there was no one there to be shocked. You couldn't count little blonde Jeanne. Terrified, white as a sheet, leaning against the bookshelves to support herself, she was on the point of fainting. I took her arm.

'We need a change of scene,' I told her. 'Let's go somewhere less crowded. Show me where the bar is. We'll feel better when we've had a brandy. Then we can hold a council of war.'

In Delan's little sitting-room, Jeanne put away a large glass of *fine* that brought some colour back to her cheeks. I went back to the office to examine the body. When I'd finished I appropriated a packet of cigarettes lying on the blotter and came back to find Jeanne feeling much better. She sat smoking the cigarette I gave her while I told her about the attack on myself and the abduction of Victor Fernèse, omitting the fact that I knew the woman involved. I learned that Jeanne had been asleep in her attic when she was awakened by the noise. Nobody had bothered to go right up there. Her room overlooked the grounds at the back, so she'd neither heard nor seen the car. She'd only come down when she realized something odd was going on.

'I believe I know how the doctor died,' I informed her. 'It was largely accidental. He was dealt a heavy blow, and as he fell he hit his head on a corner of the desk. It's made of very hard wood with a metal reinforcement. He fractured his skull and that was the end of him. The back of his head was crushed as if he'd been hit with a hammer. But he wasn't hit by a hammer. He was hit on the chin by a colossal brute who'd make our friend Pierre look like a midget . . . Where *is* Pierre, by the way?'

'He sleeps in the porter's lodge by the front door.'

'Let's go and see if he's still there.'

He wasn't. He was lying on the front steps gagged and bound. We untied him and he told us his story, serving it up as a verbal sandwich, with two oaths for every polite word. He'd gone to answer a ring at the bell, thinking it was the 'smugglers' come to pick up their clients, and found himself face to face with a masked man armed with a revolver. Before he could utter a word, the intruder coshed him so hard that he just lay there out for the count while an accomplice trussed him up.

When I informed him of his employer's sad fate he was so flabbergasted he had to pour himself another brandy – we'd gone back to the sitting-room to keep the bottle company.

'Can anyone fill me in about the patient who's been kidnapped?' I asked. Neither of them could. I went on to something else. Fred Delan's death was going to create a lot of problems. The police would probably have to be told. But would they? Pierre didn't like the idea, but didn't see what else we could do. I was about to object that it wouldn't be a very good move with the house full of people waiting to cross illegally into the Unoccupied Zone, when the telephone rang in the office where the body was lying. I rushed to answer it, followed by the male nurse. After listening for a moment I passed the receiver to him, thinking he might be able to understand better than I could the cryptic pronouncements issuing from it.

'The "river" is fordable at Saint-Alter,' announced the ex-boxer when he'd put down the phone. 'They're coming for the "cargo" at seven o'clock this morning.'

It was already well past five. As I was anxious not to miss my chance, that didn't leave much time for looking through the dead man's papers for information about the kidnapped madman. Jeanne, the male nurse and I concocted a reasonably plausible story to feed to the other people in the house about the night's events, and while the other two went off to serve it up I began my search. But I drew a blank: you couldn't count a note on a medical record card to the effect that Victor Fernèse used to be an engineer. Delan, who'd filled in the card when the patient was admitted, had failed to mention what branch of engineering was involved, so it was about as much use to me as knowing his taste in ties.

That evening, with feelings of frustration that may well be imagined, I crossed the demarcation line.

6 Having a lovely time

I arrived in Marseilles in dull weather on the afternoon of
Monday 16 November. Not wishing to go to a hotel I
thought of Jean Rouget, a friend I'd not looked up on my
previous visit but who was now going to prove very useful. I'd met him before the war, drinking at the Rhumerie
Martiniquaise. After the armistice he'd found his talent
lay in the manufacturing line. Having got out of the
Occupied Zone and settled in Marseilles, he'd started a
cooperative venture with a group of other lads as keen as
he was, for various reasons, to view the swastika from
afar. They had a factory where they made crystallized
fruits. The product was wholesome – none of their cus-
tomers had died so far – and sales were excellent. There
were about a dozen partners involved, men and women,
all from Saint-Germain-des-Prés or Montparnasse and
representing a wide variety of callings, from the cinema
to painting by way of music-hall and political agitation.
They included chemists among their number. Most
of them had names like Duval, Dubois or Dupont,
and because of this Rouget's more unscrupulous rivals
referred to him as Papa Ghetto. The Allfruit factory was
indeed a most pleasant and reputable establishment. I
went straight there.

Rouget, despite his name, is pale, with a hatchet face, large spectacles and a powerful bass voice.

'Here comes the fuzz!' he bawled, as soon as he saw me, not caring whether he caused a panic or got me lynched. 'How are you, filthy fuzz?'

'Very well,' I answered. What else can you say?

Noticing the alteration in my features, he hoped it was the result of a rough house with one of my clients. Not a bit of it, I retorted, I was dead, didn't he know? and my phiz was the phiz of a ghost. But actually I wouldn't mind a serious talk with him.

We went into his office. He asked no questions, but I did the decent thing and made up a few reasons to account for my presence in Marseilles. A quarter of an hour later he'd found a corner of the factory I could kip down in that night.

For the time being, I lingered at the Allfruit factory just long enough to renew my acquaintance with some of Rouget's colleagues and to learn that despite official optimism in the newspapers the occupation of the south coast by Axis troops had not passed off without incident. In the Vieux Port, a German officer had been shot on the very first day, and a house razed to the ground by a tank. This tranquil atmosphere should give plenty of scope for Nestor Burma's dynamism.

I set off smartly to see the mysterious Robert Beaucher.

I went up the stairs without bothering the concierge and rang at the door on the left on the second floor. It wasn't Beaucher who opened. It was a sallow, sickly looking individual with a sparse fringe of beard. He seemed to be in a dream and none too bright either.

When I asked to speak to M. Robert Beaucher his

eyes opened wide. 'Robert Beaucher? There must be some mistake. There's no one of that name here. My name's Maillard.'

'Listen, M. Maillard,' I said, inserting a foot in the door as he tried to shut it in my face. 'I was here a few days ago, visiting M. Beaucher.' I shouldered him aside and went in. There was no doubt about it: this *was* the place. Maillard, who'd been watching me closely, clapped his hand to his forehead.

'How stupid of me!' he exclaimed. 'When did you say you were here?' I told him. 'Of course!' he said. 'That was while I was away!' And he explained how, living in modest circumstances and finding he had to go away, he'd sub-let his flat to a friend for a fortnight. Perhaps 'friend' was not quite the right word. It was just someone he'd met at the Café Riche a few months back, with whom he had a few tastes and opinions in common. But now he was beginning to wonder . . . 'I haven't missed any of my personal belongings, but I knew the man you call Beaucher by another name altogether.'

'Oh? and what name was that?' He was obviously going to invent one, but I supposed I'd better look as though I believed him.

'Barnabé – Robert Barnabé,' he said.

'And when did you get back?'

'On the tenth.'

'And was Barnabé or Beaucher, or whatever, still here?'

'No, he'd gone off the previous day, according to the concierge. He left the keys with her and the rent he owed me in an envelope on the table.'

'Have you seen him since?'

'Now that's odd – I've been back to the Café Riche two or three times, but he wasn't there. I didn't think anything of it at the time, but now . . . '

'Now?'

'Well, it seems strange.'

'It *is* strange,' I told him. 'Is there anywhere apart from the Café Riche where I might get hold of him? It's very important.'

'I don't know of anywhere.'

'H'm. Well, thanks anyway, M. Maillard.'

As I went out I stopped for a few words with the concierge. I didn't learn anything except that, as I'd supposed, Maillard wasn't on the telephone. This would allow me to make an experiment, for want of anything better to do.

I went to a nearby bistro and rang Rouget to ask him to lend me his van. 'No dancing-girls required?' he wanted to know. I told him there was one involved already and that was enough. All right then, I could have the van. It arrived shortly afterwards, driven by a canny-looking cove with red hair. We took to each other immediately, and I told him where to go and got in beside him. While we waited outside Maillard's building we talked about Paris. It was getting dark and I was starting to give up hope when Maillard came out, got on a bicycle and rode away. We followed him roughly south-eastwards across the town. Soon we were in a less built-up area, where the road ran alongside a railway line.

'Where are we?'

'Somewhere between La Blancarde and Saint-Barnabé, I reckon.'

'Saint-Barnabé, eh? That's very interesting.' We continued for a while beside the railway line. The sound of the trains conveniently covered the noise of our engine. Suddenly our quarry stopped, got off his bicycle and started to wheel it along a muddy turn-off marked 'No through road' and bordered on both sides by waste ground and broken palings. Leaving my companion to look after the van, I got out and followed Maillard, or whoever he was, ducking when necessary behind the fence. It was a lonely, depressing place: the air smelled of soot, and dusk was falling. One behind the other, we finally reached two detached houses standing on the left-hand side of the track and facing another on the right. I saw Maillard stop in front of the third house. I froze. He rang the bell hanging above the gate. A frightful clanging but no response: only darkness, silence, emptiness. One of the two houses opposite was equally forbidding. The other seemed to be lived in. A faint rectangle of light appeared on the soggy patch of ground in front of it as a little old woman opened the door, poked out her head and screeched 'Puss, puss,puss!' No answer. She came out into the middle of the road, grumbling to herself. Her eye fell on Maillard, and in the intervals of calling to the cat and without lowering her voice she enquired, 'Is it M. Bernard you want, sir?'

So! here he called himself Bernard! In under an hour Beaucher had been referred to by three different names!

'Yes,' answered his visitor, 'but he doesn't appear to be in.'

The old woman seemed to be deaf. She repeated her question and Maillard yelled back 'YES!'

'He's not there! Must be away! I've not seen or heard anything of him for days.'

She resumed her search for the cat while Maillard came to stand in the light to write a message in a notebook. He tore off the sheet, then went and put it into the mail box on Beaucher-Barnabé-Bernard's gate. Meanwhile the driver of the van had edged it up stealthily to join me. He didn't want to miss the show. He was a film fan and because of pressure of work at Allfruit's he hadn't been to the cinema for three weeks. He thought he might make up for lost thrills if he stuck with me. How right he was.

Having kindly if unwittingly led me to my ex-client's real address, Maillard went off, still wheeling his bicycle. Accompanied by Ginger, I set about taking a closer look at the house. The old woman, puss or no puss, had gone back into the warm. But just as my companion and I were about to come out of hiding, another cyclist appeared from nowhere, jolting intrepidly back along the bumpy track which Maillard had negotiated on foot. We hung on a bit in case there was another one coming and we could make up a four for bridge, then went over to the house.

From the outside it looked as if it had only four rooms, two upstairs and two down, without attic or garage. There was no garden except at the front, where a meagre strip of ground was planted with shrubs. The gate creaked as I pushed it open, and I couldn't help jogging the bell into action. Luckily there seemed to be no one for miles around except the deaf old woman, and no one came to see who was making all the noise. I extracted Maillard's note from the mail box on the gate and then shone my torch on to the abnormally loud bell. It was very large and, unlike the rusty chain attached to it, brand new.

The house door was latched but not locked. I picked it open, under the curious eye of my driver, and we went in. We found ourselves in a narrow passage lit, when I'd found the switch, by a weak bulb hanging from the ceiling. At the far end of the passage was a staircase. Two doors opened off the hall, one leading into the kitchen, the other into a larger living room, into which we went, turning on the light.

'Well, blow me!' gasped Ginger.

No wonder nothing had been heard lately from Robert Beaucher-Barnabé-Bernard! He was stretched out on the floor, stiff as a corpse. Which was what he was. The body was beginning to whiff.

There was no knife or bullet wound. It looked as if he'd suddenly been taken ill, tried to hold on to the mantelpiece and fallen with his feet in the fireplace. He was wearing a dressing-gown, trousers, socks and sandals. The fire must have been still alight when he fell with his feet in the hearth, and there wasn't much left of his shoes and socks. The feet too had been badly burned, and a bit of the flimsy dressing-gown. It was lucky the whole house hadn't gone up in flames. He couldn't have suffered any pain from the fire, though: he must have been dead before he fell, or he'd have moved his feet away from the live coals.

The window was closed and shuttered and we'd seen no one about, but just in case anyone should notice chinks of light I told my companion to hang the tablecloth over it. I saw then that there was a nearly empty bottle of alcohol on the table.

My ex-client was wearing a jacket under his dressing-gown. I went through the pockets but found only the usual insignificant odds and ends. There was nothing in the wallet to indicate who he really was. The identity and ration cards were in the name of Robert Bernard, aged forty, born in Eure, occupation: journalist – the ideal cover for someone with no particular profession. In a pocket of the dressing-gown I found what felt like a soft object wrapped in a sheet of cheap writing paper. When I opened it, out fell a piece of yellow material in the shape of a six-pointed star, with the word *Jew* written in pseudo-Hebraic characters in the middle. The star of

David, which Jews are compelled to wear in the Occupied Zone. Scrawled on the paper was a message: *The Nazis are coming, you dirty Yid. Now you'll have to wear this.* There was no signature. I remembered the other note, left by Maillard in the mail box, and hastily looked to see what it said: *Your bird's husband's getting suspicious. He came to see me. He's after you.* The handwriting and tone of the two notes were completely different, but both were unsigned, if you didn't count the peculiar scrawl at the end of the second one. *The Lynx*, it said. I put both papers in my pocket.

'Tell me,' I said to my driver, 'did many Jews commit suicide when they knew the Germans had come?' He wrenched his eyes away from the corpse and said yes, there had been quite a few. Had this one . . . ?

'Yes. The post-mortem will show he died of poison, probably cyanide. It's difficult to get hold of, but everyone knows the Jews can always wangle things. Do you think that, too?'

'Everyone says so,' he agreed.

'Yes, and a very convenient opinion it is, too. But this Jew was even smarter than the others. He managed to conceal the fact that he belonged to the chosen race, and the word "Jew" doesn't appear on his identity card. So he was terrified when, just as the Germans were coming, some unknown enemy discovered his secret and threatened to give him away. He had a few drinks to bolster his courage and then he swallowed his tablet. He fell down near the fireplace in convulsions and rolled on to the fire, scattering the logs but not putting it out. He was already dead when his feet got burned . . . Why are you gawping at him like that? You don't seem to be able to take your eyes off him!'

He took off his cap and ran his fingers through his

flaming hair. 'I think I've seen him somewhere before.'

'Where?'

'I can't remember. Of course, I may be wrong, but I don't think so.'

'Well, let me know if you remember. In the meantime, what do you think of my little reconstruction of the death-scene?'

'You sounded like a rozzer showing off!'

'You mean a proper policeman? Not just a private eye?'

'No, a real one.'

'I reason like a real detective! You've made my day!'

We rummaged round the ground floor and found precisely nothing. One of the upstairs rooms was used for storage, the other was a bedroom. In the first there was a bench and tools that had recently been used for some amateur locksmith's work. The whole place was untidy. There was no trace of any feminine touch: the absence of dust betokened rather the obsession of a fussy bachelor. It looked as though Beaucher the industrialist alias Bernard the journalist was no more a married man with a family than I was an archdeacon. That was my only interesting discovery.

Suddenly Ginger looked at his watch. 'We ought to be making tracks – it's nearly nine. The extended curfew they imposed after that business in the Vieux Port is still on for another day. We don't want to meet any patrols. I hate having to show my papers, I've got a thing about it.'

'Me too,' I said. 'Let's go.' Anyway there was nothing to stay for. As we were leaving I noticed a set of keys hanging from a nail by the front door. One of them fitted the lock itself, while the second, which was flat and very small, was for the extra bolt above it. The third was for the front gate. The doormat was still damp from where we'd wiped our muddy feet. As we went through the front gate I tried not to jangle the bell, but it was fixed in such a way that this was impossible. Again, though, nobody came to investigate.

It was raining. We were soaked by the time we reached the car. And the place had livened up. As we approached the main road we saw it was jammed with army vehicles going towards the city.

'We're going to get caught like rats in a trap!' groaned my companion. 'We'll never be able to get through this lot – we'll have to wait till it's gone past. And these convoys can go on for ever!' But the words were hardly out of his mouth when the last vehicle swept past and we could emerge on to the road and follow behind the Wehrmacht almost as if we were part of the convoy.

It was raining harder than ever. 'How long have you been having this filthy weather?' I asked. 'It was chilly when I was here on the eighth, but at least it was dry.'

'It started on Friday the thirteenth.' He gave a sarcastic laugh. 'Blame it on God or the Germans!'

7 Bring on the dancing-girls

When we got back to Allfruit Rouget was sitting before the remains of a meal, nervously smoking a cigarette and talking to a charming brunette. He was starting to get worried. When we appeared he gave a huge sigh of relief, his brow cleared and he resumed his usual jocular manner.

'This is Olga,' he told me. 'The dancer you turned down earlier on.'

'That wasn't very gallant,' she teased.

Suddenly Ginger uttered an exclamation. 'Oh! I remember now where I saw the corpse!'

Rouget started. 'What corpse?'

'The one we saw just now.'

I sat down to explain, first giving a meaning look at the girl. It was intercepted by Ginger. 'You can talk in front of her,' he said. 'And in any case you'll have to put her in the picture, because she knows Bernard.'

I could hardly believe my luck. 'I'm beginning to think I did the right thing, coming to Allfruit. Whatever's needed, you can produce it. You wouldn't have something to eat and drink, would you?'

We were promptly supplied, and after swearing the others to secrecy I served them up a cock-and-bull story with just enough truth in it to make it plausible.

'So, Mademoiselle Olga,' I said when I'd finished eating and was pouring myself some more wine, 'you knew this chap Bernard?'

Her answer made my drink go down the wrong way. 'I know Jackie Lamour, too!'

'I told you she's a dancer,' Rouget reminded me. 'She's one of the girls at the Blackbird Club.'

'I *was* one of them,' she corrected. 'Now, because of the lousy curfew, the place has closed down.'

'We'll see if we can find you another job,' said I. 'In the meantime, tell me what you know about Jackie Lamour and Bernard.'

'Well,' she began, 'Bernard often came to the cabaret. When he wasn't out front with the other clients he was in Jackie's dressing-room. They seemed very thick.' She paused. 'I suppose we *are* talking about the same man? What's your Beaucher alias Bernard like?' I described him. 'That's the one all right. He looked a bit like a Jew.'

I laughed. 'Yes, a bit.'

'No mistake about it,' said Ginger. 'I met him once or twice backstage at the Blackbird.'

'Well, that's him identified,' I said. 'Carry on, baby.'

'That's all. I don't know any more. Except that he and Jackie fell out recently.'

'Fell out? Why?' And to get her to speed it up a bit I added, 'I've a feeling there's going to be big money in this case, and you'll be in on it.'

This did the trick – the words came pouring out. 'It's like this. Jackie's a terrible shrew, always moaning about something, and she treats us girls like dirt. Well, the other day, the seventh of November it was, she gets a cold, so she goes on earlier than usual, when there's hardly anyone in the audience, rushes through her number at top speed and then goes home. And the boss gives us girls a telling off as if it was our fault.'

'And Bernard went with her, did he?'

'Yes, he'd been with her practically the whole evening. She didn't come in the next day, and the boss had another row with us. He was livid – he thought she might have gone to work for one of his rivals. He sent someone round to her place, but she wasn't there. He led us an awful life until the tenth, when he calmed down again because he'd got his star back. But she was in a foul temper. Never stopped grumbling.'

'In front of you?'

'No, in her dressing-room, ticking off her dresser and so on. But the walls are paper-thin and I could hear.'

'What was she mad about?'

'I didn't take much notice of the first part – it was just the usual moaning only much more violent. She seemed terribly edgy. No wonder, as it turned out! I couldn't help laughing when I knew!' She was hugging herself at the thought.

'What do you mean by "the first part"?'

'The first lot of grumbling – at her dresser. The second part was the good bit, and to think I might have missed it! . . . I'd better explain. When I finished work that night I could have come straight back here, but let me warn you: there's no chance of getting a good night's sleep here. While half this lot are snoring their heads off, the other half are shouting the odds about dialectical materialism. Anyway, when I finished work that evening I was done in, so I thought I'd have a snooze in my dressing-room until the Club closed. After all, Jackie couldn't make as much noise as a Marxist philosopher! I switched off the light, lay down and fell asleep. I was woken up by Jackie next door yelling at André, who'd just gone in. He's one of her pals, some sort of gangster or black marketeer, always hanging round her and Bernard. I could hear most of what they were saying – she thought they were alone and she was beside herself with rage. "I've got something to tell you", she began. "We've been had good and proper! It wasn't the wog who stole back the stuff he'd sold me – it was Bernard!"

"'Bernard?" says André. "But Bernard was with you!"

"'He may have been with me," she hisses, "but how do you explain the fact that he's going round with the banknotes that were pinched from my safe?" This really gets to André and he lets out a string of juicy oaths. "Yes," she says, "we were having tea somewhere and I saw one of my thousand-franc notes in his wallet when he paid the bill." When André points out that there are quite a few thousand-franc notes about, she just lets fly at him. "Anyway," she ends up, "I could tell, because I'd written down the numbers. I'm right, you'll see if I'm not!" André said something I didn't understand and she seemed to calm down a bit. I couldn't hear the rest of the conversation properly because they lowered their voices. I waited until they'd gone before leaving myself. There, that's all. Is it any use to you?'

It certainly was! I also got her to tell me what André looked like, but the description didn't fit anyone I knew. I stood up.

'Thanks, Olga, you're a great girl! May I kiss you?'

'Ooh!', she simpered, 'I don't know if I ought to let you! You're a married man!'

'Married! Who says I'm married?'

'What about the wedding ring?' She pointed to the third finger of my left hand. Laughing, I twisted my signet-ring round so that the stone was showing. 'Oh well, in that case . . . ', she said.

I gave her a kiss. It was only the fifteenth that day, she told me.

Attagirl, Olga!

8 Brain work

In a corner of a large storeroom, surrounded by fragrant sacks of dried figs and dates, I lay down on my mattress, lit a pipe and settled down to think. This imbroglio was beginning to make sense. Here's roughly how I saw it:

Bernard, who had told me a pack of lies about himself, was a close acquaintance of shady Jackie Lamour. She had some letters that he wanted to get hold of without her knowing. He thought the best thing would be to arrange for someone else to take them, and then on the day of the theft stick close to Jackie all the time so as to have a perfect alibi. The proxy thief was to be Nestor Burma. Why me? First, because I had a reputation for being more of a daredevil than some of my colleagues. Second, I lived in Paris, virtually in a foreign country now that France was cut in two by the demarcation line. Whatever might happen later, once the job was done and I'd gone home I'd know nothing more about it.

Bernard's plan was a bit rough and ready but it could have been worse. The fact that he had to call on my services showed he was on his own, with no one else he could ask to help him. Maillard, it was true, had lent him his flat for our first meeting so that he wouldn't have to ask me to his own place, a precaution as necessary on

Jackie's account as on mine, but Maillard didn't look to me as if he was good for much else. Just the same, I decided that in the morning I'd pay him another visit. His fibs suggested a connection with the other liars in the case.

As for the letters that Beaucher-Barnabé-Bernard had paid me to pinch, what exactly were they? Of course, I knew by now they weren't just ordinary love-letters. Under the ardent declarations was hidden some sort of dynamite, judging by the harm they'd already caused. I couldn't think why I hadn't seen it from the outset. The padlocked windows and new bolts at the villa at Cap Croisette should have alerted me – without the keys made for me by B-B-B I'd never have got in. People don't take precautions like those for love-letters, even if they do have blackmailing potential. I'd read them over and over again, but could I remember them now? I gave up. I'd do better to test a certain theory I had. But thoughts about letters – was it because they were supposed to be love-letters? – had led to thoughts about secretaries, and I resolved to send an interzone card to Hélène next day to let her know I was all right. I only hoped *she* was all right too.

Back to my cogitations. When I'd handed the letters over to B-B-B, I'd caught the train for Paris. On the same train there was another passenger, Sdenko Matich the Croat, who bore a physical and sartorial resemblance to myself. The 'wog', as Jackie called him, had met his death on that journey. At that point I had an idea – my instinct told me it was on target. I'd been thinking that as an extra precaution B-B-B had sent a hit man to eliminate me and that he'd got the wrong man and shot the Croat. But what if it was the other way round, and *it was I who'd been taken for the Croat*? To make this easier to follow, let's suppose he was in cahoots with B-B-B and Jackie. That would explain why B-B-B had seemed so amused at our first meeting and why the dancer had thought Matich was the burglar. She hadn't had time to look at me closely before I hit her, and anyway my hat was pulled down over my eyes. Yes, it all seemed to fit. When Jackie came to she was furious. She'd known that the letters had gone because she'd checked straight away. Bernard told me she hadn't noticed, but I knew by now how much what *he* said was worth. I was sure I was right. She'd checked on the letters, seen through the 'burglary' trick and the alibi and was out for revenge. Could it have been she who killed the Croat? Why not? She wasn't at home on the night of the 8 November – the night the Croat was murdered – or the next day. And the medical evidence showed he was shot from in front, possibly by someone he knew and trusted. What would her motive have been? She wanted to punish him – my impression so far had been that she was a humourless, irascible, vindictive woman. Still, death was rather an extreme punishment for the theft of a few thousand-franc notes, so she must have killed him to get back the other things he'd stolen. That was why Matich had no luggage when he got to Paris. But why kill him in the Occupied Zone? Jackie must have known his movements and where he lived in Marseilles. Surely she could have done it there? Well, I supposed, the opportunity didn't arise. Unless . . . unless there was another reason.

The more I thought about it the more convinced I was that the bundle of letters with its black ribbon outside and smutty allusions within was in its way more dangerous than a high-explosive bomb. The stakes must be very high. The murderer wouldn't want the body to be found on her own patch: if it could be discovered in Paris, cut off as it was by the demarcation line, that would give her a breathing space. Also, if she wanted to keep a distance between herself and the corpse, she wouldn't have stayed on the train until it reached the terminus but got off somewhere along the line. I remembered La Haute-Futaie, where at present, as frequent travellers knew, the trains always slackened speed. Being a dancer she was light and nimble – she could have jumped from the train while it was moving slowly. She might have had a bolt-hole in the neighbourhood – she could even still be there, since the last time I'd seen her she was in the Occupied Zone. That's where I ought to have been now, instead of lying here theorizing on a lumpy mattress in a Marseilles sweet factory, if I hadn't been so anxious to interview the so-called Monsieur Beaucher.

But I'd believed Beaucher had tried to play me a really dirty trick. Also, after the clinic episode, I'd needed to see him in order to extract some information about Jackie Lamour's intriguing nocturnal activities. So I'd come to Marseilles, discovered he'd given me a false address, traced him to the right one, and then what? I stumble over his dead body and find someone has got there before me, asked their questions and finished up by giving him a dose of cyanide. Because of course his death was nothing to do with yellow stars, taunts of 'dirty Jew', or fear of Hitler's anti-Semitic French henchmen. B-B-B had simply been bumped off. I'd had my suspicions all along. Now Olga had confirmed them, and even helped put me on to the possible murderers.

According to our chorus girl, Jackie had returned to the Blackbird Club on the tenth, grumpier than ever. First because she had, of course, found nothing in the Croat's luggage. Second, the announcement of my death had suggested to her that the real thief might be Matich's look-alike, Nestor Burma. She knew which one of us she'd killed, but she wondered what had been going on. And third, she knew now that Bernard was mixed up in the theft, because she'd seen him with some of the money stolen from her safe. He'd ignored my naïve suggestion about seeing she got it back before she called in the police: he knew she'd no more do that than fly in the air. I wondered incidentally what there was about the famous banknote to enable her to identify that particular one. But I had more pressing things to think of.

When Nestor Burma came on the scene in the role of the deceased Croat, and Bernard turned out to have been conning her, Jackie put two and two together and concluded that the private detective had been hired by Bernard to purloin the letters, and been mistaken by her at the time for Matich. And those letters she'd travelled so far and committed murder to find were here in Marseilles at Bernard's place. So a little visit was in order, even if only to make sure she wasn't mistaken about the thousand-franc note.

As for the perpetrators of the crime in the lonely house at Saint-Barnabé, I'd no proof of who they were, but this was what seemed to have happened:

Suicide I'd always thought dubious for the following reasons:

(a) The floors and furniture had been almost free of dust. Though everything else in the house proclaimed that a bachelor lived there, there wasn't a speck to be seen. So close to a railway, this was extraordinary. Intending suicides have been known to do strange things before carrying out their plan, but I couldn't see B-B-B, if one assumed he'd been terrified by the threatening letter left so conveniently on his corpse, going round doing the housework before he took the fatal pill. The suspicious absence of dust showed that someone else had been there and carefully removed all traces of their presence.

(b) The doors were unlocked, though B-B-B might have been expected to secure them. The criminals couldn't lock up behind them unless they took the keys out with them, which would have destroyed the scenario they'd set up.

(c) Only part of the dressing-gown had been consumed by the fire, yet it was made of a material that would normally go up in flames, burn rapidly and set the house alight in the process.

This, therefore, was my version of events:

The criminals tied up their victim, being careful not to leave any marks on his skin. They then put their questions to him, and when he didn't answer held his feet in the fire. He would have screamed, of course, but as it was a lonely spot and the only neighbour was deaf, they could play their little games without worrying about the noise. Whether B-B-B talked I couldn't say; in the end, whether he'd been a good boy or not, he got a cyanide sweet.

The murderers then untied the body and arranged it to look as if the victim had fallen in the fireplace accidentally in the course of some kind of convulsion. The burns to the feet suffered after death masked the marks left by the torture. They completed the effect by burning a bit of the dressing-gown and planting the 'motive' – the anonymous letter and the yellow star – in the jacket pocket. Then they cleaned the entire house. They may even have searched it if B-B-B hadn't told them anything, but the place was in such a mess it was difficult to tell whether it had been searched or not – if it had, it was a clumsy job. But they'd set the scene hoping it would lead to the interpretation I gave Ginger. The authorities would see no need for a lengthy investigation: just another Jew who'd committed suicide. Nothing to worry about. As in the case of the Croat, the murderers would have a breathing space.

I still didn't know whether B-B-B had told them where he'd hidden the letters which were certainly the stake being played for in this tragic encounter. Another puzzle was Jackie Lamour's abduction of the mental patient. Were the two things connected? Who was Victor Fernèse?

By now I was beginning to suspect everyone in the case of going under a false name. Certainly a large proportion of them did, starting with myself, Nestor Burma alias Monsieur Martin. Beaucher was also Bernard, and even that wasn't all, while Jackie Lamour must be a stage name. Even the little chorus girl's handle sounded like something out of a popular novel. Is anyone ever called Olga in real life? In fact, Rouget was the only one so far using his real name. Maillard, now – was he really called Maillard?

Maillard and Olga were drowsily confused in my mind. As I twisted my loose ring, a funny thought occurred to me, though that's only a figure of speech – for Maillard himself it might be no laughing matter. When I remembered the noisy bell of the house at Saint-Barnabé, it made me think B-B-B hadn't talked, and Maillard might be going to learn the hard way not to go warning Don Juans that deceived husbands were on their track. I told myself I'd go and find out first thing in the morning.

I was gradually falling asleep. All kinds of images drifted before my eyes as if in a film. I saw Hélène and wondered if it wasn't dangerous to ask her to find out about Victor Fernèse, and anyway where should I tell her to go and look? At Fred Delan's clinic? The trouble was I was both hunter and hunted, my movements were hampered – but could I ask a girl to get involved in this mess? I'd been asked to get the letters back, I'd done so and been paid thirty thousand francs for my services. But I'd better give it up now. One thought led to another: what was so special about the thousand-franc note that gave B-B-B away to Jackie Lamour? I gave such a start I bumped my head on a sack of figs.

I'd had a terrifying thought. In due course, after I'd stolen the dancer's money, I'd put it away in my wallet with my own. When I gave it back to Beaucher I must have mixed up the actual notes and kept at least one of hers – the one I paid Boris the make-up man with. For it had been cut in two and mended with sticky tape. Cut cleanly with scissors. That was common practice in certain circles. When someone was doing a job they were paid half the money – in half-notes – in advance, and the other half when the mission was completed. This was done in all the secret services. At the time I hadn't looked closely at what I'd assumed was the usual scruffy old paper money. Now, with all these murders involved, I saw it in a different light. I wanted nothing to do with any secret service, thank you very much! Wild horses wouldn't make me go on with this case.

I was in a considerable state by now, but the combined effect of experiencing a revelation and making a decision was soporific: I fell fast asleep.

9 A quiet street

I was too nervous to sleep well and woke at 6.30. I lit a pipe and smoked it slowly to clear my brain. Then I sat up and got thinking. I didn't feel like dancing a jig but I was in less of a blue funk than I'd been the night before. Working on this case was like being in a powder magazine where a lot of drunks were going round with lighted candles, but I couldn't deny that it interested me strangely. I said this to myself several times and then got up. People were coming and going in the factory and one of them showed me where I could wash. Then I went to see Rouget.

'I want to go back to Paris as soon as possible,' I told him. 'Illegally, of course. You must know a way – I can't use the one I came by.' He did know a way, but it couldn't be arranged just like that. If I could wait until the evening he'd be able to give me an address.

To pass the time I went out for a stroll. It had stopped raining, and the sun was even making half-hearted attempts to compete with the mistral. I tossed up whether to write to Hélène but decided it wasn't necessary since I'd soon be in Paris. I went into a bistro.

It was no good, I couldn't keep my mind off those

letters. I tried listening to the conversation of the other people leaning on the counter, then watching as they rolled dice to decide who should pay for the next round. But my thoughts always came back to the letters. Perhaps they were only a decoy to divert attention from the real reason for all that carnage? But I devoutly hoped they were as important as I'd thought, partly to preserve my theory and partly for another reason . . .

After my third white wine I thought I'd go and spend a restful day in a continuous performance cinema, but I'd forgotten: there was a war on, and I couldn't find one. Several times I was on the point of going to call on M. Maillard, but then I remembered I'd promised myself to stop playing with fire. Then . . . a little voice murmured that this would be the first time Nestor Burma had chickened out. And anyway I was already walking down the street where Maillard lived: the old pins had decided the matter by themselves. Who said private sleuthing's all brain work?

I rang the bell. No one answered. I rang again. Still no answer. I could tell when I rattled the door that it was locked. It looked as if the lock wouldn't be difficult to pick, but that could wait. I went back downstairs.

When I'd arrived the concierge had hidden herself away in her lodge, but now she was sloshing water round the hallway, pretending to be washing the floor. In answer to my question she told me she hadn't seen Maillard go out – nor heard him come in the previous night for that matter. He must have been caught by the curfew and hauled off to the police station, where he probably still was.

I needed to do some checking at Saint-Barnabé so I took myself back to Allfruit and borrowed a bicycle. If I was in trouble, sticking my head in the sand wasn't going to help. This case might be dangerous, but it fascinated me, and I might as well carry on until I got hurt, when at least I'd have a good excuse for giving up.

The street of the three houses, one of them the scene of a murder, was no pleasanter in daylight than it had been at dusk or in the dark. It was still squalid and noisy from the trains, and the air still stank of coal-dust and smoke. In that polluted atmosphere no one would have noticed the smell of scorching flesh. Outside the house where the deaf old woman lived, a cat sat on the windowsill licking its fur with a nimble pink tongue, starting nervously every time an engine whistle screeched. There was no garden. The front door opened straight on to the street. I knocked and the old woman appeared.

I asked if I could come in – I didn't want the conversation broadcast for miles around. The room was sparsely furnished but clean. In the place of honour on the sideboard stood photographs of two youngish men bearing a marked resemblance to each other and to the old woman. The laborious exchange that followed left me hoarse but pleased with my little harvest of information.

I said I was a pal of B-B-B's just arrived from Paris. I was supposed to be meeting some other friends at his house and then we were all going on to Cannes, but there seemed to be nobody at home. Of course, I was a bit late: I'd been held up by red tape when I was crossing the line.

The old woman sang Bernard's praises – he was such a nice neighbour! – and yes, he'd been gone for several days. He'd had visitors recently. When? Oh, that was the day Minou went missing again, the little tinker, and she'd had to go out looking for him. That was how she happened to see the visitors across the road, because as a rule she spent most of her time in the kitchen. It was on the twelfth, when it was starting to get dark, and she was sure of the date because it was the last fine day before all that awful rain. The Midi, land of sunshine, indeed!

'Yes, that'll have been my friends,' I said. 'There was a woman with them, wasn't there?'

'That's right, monsieur. There were three of them, two men and a woman. That was a lot of people for a quiet street like this where no one ever comes. A cul-de-sac they call it. Nobody lives here but me and M. Bernard, and M. Bernard never has any visitors. And who'd visit the house next door? It's to let, but everyone knows it's practically falling down. Holes in the ceilings, the floors, the walls – everywhere! And all this way out! The refugees from the Occupied Zone would rather sleep five to a room in a hotel, or even in the street, than trek out here to the back of beyond. It's different for us – we're used to it.'

When she paused for breath I asked her if she'd mind describing Bernard's visitors on the twelfth – then I could see whether it *was* my friends or not.

'Well, it was getting dark and my eyes aren't what they were. I can't tell you much about your friends, if it was them. The lady looked like a fashion model, that's all I noticed.'

Like a tart, she means, I thought, but she doesn't like to use the word about a friend of mine. Jackie Lamour must have been here on the twelfth. Aloud, I said I was sure now who the visitors were, and she added that another gentleman had called there yesterday. He'd come and stood in front of her door, where he'd be able to see to write a note, and she remembered he had a funny little beard. I said no, it didn't sound like anyone I knew, and started to walk to the door, stopping in front of the photographs.

'A couple of fine lads,' I said. 'I take it they're your sons?'

'Yes, sir,' she said proudly. 'The older one's married – he was taken prisoner by the Germans. The other one, Jean, managed not to get caught. He lives here with me – I don't know how I'd manage without him.'

'What does he do?'

'He works for Daumas-Aragno at La Joliette.' I'd never heard of Daumas-Aragno, but I knew where La Joliette was.

'That's quite a distance,' I said. 'I suppose he goes by bike?'

'Oh no!' she cried. 'He walks to the stop and takes the tram. When he's on nights he goes all the way on foot. A bicycle costs the earth nowadays – if you can find one. No, he hasn't got a bike.'

I thanked her, groused a bit because my friends hadn't waited for me, and told her I thought I'd take a stroll round the neighbourhood. She said I could leave my bicycle in her shed and just pick it up myself when I was ready.

I walked to where the road ended in a broken-down wall, and stood for a moment looking at the desolate landscape beyond before retracing my steps as far as the house that was to let. I stepped through a gap in the fence and made my way across the rubbish-strewn ground to the side of the dilapidated building. It looked even worse by daylight than it had the last time. There were three side windows, two on the upper floor and one downstairs. Heavy iron shutters were firmly secured over the ground-floor window. All the glass in the two upstairs windows was broken. One of them was minus a shutter, the other had none – they were lying on the ground beneath.

I continued round until I came to a wooden door standing ajar. I pushed it open and stepped into an unfurnished kitchen. The room wasn't stuffy, but it smelt, like the atmosphere outside, of smoke and coal. The window was open inside, and air could get in through the slits in the shutters. Bits of plaster from the ceiling lay all over the floor. Closing the door behind me I switched on my torch and went into the passage. Faded paper dangled in strips from the damp walls. The floor was covered in dust, with patches of what looked like mud, and – I gave a whistle of satisfaction – on top of the dust and mud there were the unmistakable traces of bicycle tyres. I examined them closely.

As I stood up, the beam of my torch fell on a metal object lying under the staircase that rose in the gloom at the end of the passage. It was a muddy old bicycle with one wheel buckled as if it had been in a collision. The pattern of the tyres didn't match the marks on the floor.

With the stairs creaking under my weight I climbed to the upper floor, nearly coming to grief once over a missing tread. Three rickety doors opened on to the landing, which was lit by a skylight. The middle door led into a recess used as a lumber-room. In the room on the right, which was pitch dark, there was a strong musty smell. It was empty. I went into the room on the left.

This was the one whose windows I'd seen from the side of the house. In addition to those two there was a third overlooking B-B-B's house opposite. Its panes and shutters were gone and it had been boarded up, but there was enough space between the planks to see everything that happened outside, and the room could have been used as an observation post. Someone in fact must have been watching there. By the light flooding through the two side windows – I no longer needed my torch – I saw standing in one corner on the floor a stock of tins of food and bottles of wine, some empty, some still unused. Nearby, someone had made up a bed out of newspapers and blankets. And between the improvised larder and the makeshift bed, lying among the dirty cans and the cigarette ash, with a silk scarf and a handkerchief knotted together and lying on the floor beside him . . .

Nothing I'd seen so far today had surprised me, but I hadn't expected this. That's to say I hadn't expected to find him *here*.

His wrists and ankles were bound, his clothes dirty and his hands and face not much better, with mud even in his wispy beard. It was M. Maillard in person, and he was stiff as a board.

The old woman was right. It certainly was quiet round here. As silent as the grave.

10 Not so quiet as all that

Cautiously I examined the body. There was no money or papers in the pockets. Lifting the head by the hair, I saw a contusion at the base of the skull that looked like the result of a violent blow. You didn't need to be a genius to guess what had happened.

Maillard had been attacked, then bound and gagged and brought here. His assailant, knowing the old woman's son was at home and would hear any noise his victim made, even if she couldn't, had left in place, and probably even tightened, the gag he'd made from the scarf and handkerchief. Maillard, his breathing thus constricted, had died of suffocation during the night: he'd been dead some nine or ten hours judging by the degree of rigor mortis.

Why had he been attacked? Another easy one: because he'd rung B-B-B's bell. After the interrogation – a useless exercise, I was sure – and the subsequent killing, a member of the gang of torturers had been stationed in the empty house with orders to watch for any strangers who might come along, follow them and find out whether they were mixed up in B-B-B's dirty tricks. This explained why the old bell had been replaced by a new and louder one, rigged up so as to make such a row if anyone moved the gate that the lookout was bound to hear it even if he dozed off.

When Maillard came the previous day the lookout chased off at once in pursuit – he was the man on the bicycle Ginger and I had nearly bumped into. His bike – which had made the tracks I'd noticed – had been left ready in the passage downstairs. The one I'd seen, the one with the buckled wheel, was Maillard's – it had been brought back here with the inert body of its owner. For, I reasoned, the person trailing him, afraid of losing in the dark the only person to call at B-B-B's house since his death on the twelfth, had thought it best to grab him and have done with it. He must have had a nasty surprise when he woke up in the morning and saw the effect of his tight gag. This guy wouldn't be answering any questions now! I concluded from the empty pockets that the over-zealous crook had gone off with the victim's wallet to report to someone with a bit more sense than he had.

This case was getting more intriguing by the minute – but more dangerous too. Lives were of no account to these people. The stakes in the game must be very high and the players were vicious – I could do with a revolver in my pocket. I'd thought it better to leave my own gun behind before crossing the line, and now I felt naked. The unofficial tenant of this ruin had had to leave in a hurry and would probably be back. I wasn't averse to having a talk with him – I might learn something interesting – and a revolver would have got the conversation going nicely. However, as all I had with me was my pipe, and for all I knew the other chap might be seven feet tall and several stones heavier than me, I'd better make a strategic withdrawal and come back more suitably equipped. I'd be surprised if the folks at

Allfruit, who didn't seem all that law-abiding, couldn't rustle up a cannon, a flame-thrower or a light tank to help me out.

So with a quizzical nod at Maillard, who'd still have been in the land of the living if he hadn't led me up the garden, I went out on to the landing. As I did so I heard people talking downstairs. I hadn't heard them come in – now I couldn't get out unseen. Their voices sounded louder: they were coming towards the stairs. I looked round for somewhere to hide. There was no cover in the empty rooms. With no other choice I pushed open the door of the little lumber cupboard. It creaked horribly and I broke into a sweat: now I was really on the spot! At the same instant there was a crash followed by a string of oaths. One of the intruders had tripped over the missing tread and fallen headlong on the stairs, making such a racket they hadn't heard the creaking door. I heaved a sigh of relief.

It was dark in the cupboard but I could see the landing through cracks in the door, and the partition was thin enough for me to hear every word that might be said in the room where Maillard's body lay. Instead of forcing their secrets out of the two men now standing on the landing I could just listen in to what they said. A repulsive looking pair they were, too, their lack of natural beauty enhanced by scowls of annoyance. One of them – the one who'd been doing gymnastics on the stairs – was angrily dusting his smart overcoat and the knees of his trousers, cursing vigorously the while. He was a large man – I wouldn't have fancied taking him on, except from behind with a mallet in my hand.

The other one, the lookout, was wearing a light-coloured cap and looked nearer my class as regards weight.

'There he is,' said the author of Maillard's sad fate. 'You'll probably say I brought you all this way for nothing, but I wanted you to see him.'

'I suppose you wanted to make sure,' growled the other, 'but I needn't have bothered coming out here and breaking my neck: I've never seen him before, either.'

'Well, I don't think he's the type to have been in cahoots with Bernard. Look at him! A proper simp!'

'All stiffs have that innocent air. Still, I'm inclined to agree with you. A solid citizen, from the look of him.'

'He was poor but he was honest, as they say – you can tell by his flat.'

'Oh yes,' sneered the big man, 'I was forgetting you'd been showing some initiative!'

'Shut up, Dédé, there's no need to take the rise! Wait till Jackie gets here before you start criticizing. You think you're the only one with initiative! I had the bloke's address and his keys – I wasn't going to wait till you'd finished having it off with your black girl before I went to have a look round.'

'That'll do! I wasn't there when you came this morning because I was out seeing the big shot, and getting bawled out. He arrived last night. When I got in there was a note asking me to contact him at once. He's a man in a hurry.'

'Oh, so he's come?'

'Yes; he's staying at the Moderne, incognito, as you'd expect. That's no problem: he hasn't got a foreign accent. So listen, Paul – now he's here, no more daft mistakes. The money's waiting for us and he's been told to pay us in pounds and dollars – what do you think of that, eh? But he's going to want something in exchange, and he doesn't strike me as the sort you can keep hanging about. My God, I hope Jackie shows up soon, and that she'll be able to get something out of the loony, and quick.'

'P-pounds and dollars?' said Paul, seemingly staggered.

'Yes, pounds and dollars. Didn't expect that, did you!' Dédé sniggered. 'He can't think much of his own currency. Anyway, that's how it is, and very nice too!'

'My God, when I think that if it wasn't for that rat Bernard . . . ' and there followed a combined assault on the character of the traitor who'd taken the bread out of their mouths and made extra work for them. Then I heard them open a bottle of wine, which they passed to and fro between them as they came back to the subject of Maillard.

'Well,' said Dédé, 'did you find anything at his place then?'

'I looked everywhere but there wasn't a thing. He didn't have much anyway, just books and magazines lying around and in an old sideboard. Cheap adventure stories mostly, bought second-hand. Drawings, too, with his name on them . . . like the ones I showed you in his notebook. He was a bit of an artist.'

'He had the beard for it!'

'But there was nothing to link him with Bernard.'

'Was *he* an accountant too?'

'Yes, according to his papers. Out of work, though – he'd got an allowance book. He had a small army pension, too. God! I wonder how he came to know Bernard? The more I look at him the less he looks the part.'

'You did a proper search?'

'Here are the keys, go and look for yourself if you don't trust me! I went over that flat inch by inch – I even shook the pages of the books!'

'All right, don't get excited!'

They started muttering together, Dédé worrying in case Paul had been seen going into Maillard's flat and the other answering that he saw no one on the stairs coming or going, and that the concierge must have been out queuing somewhere. Whence I deduced that Paul Pry's visit to Maillard's flat must have taken place after mine. Then, after a short silence, Paul asked, 'What do we do now?'

'We hang around,' answered Dédé. 'I'll be glad when Jackie gets back – she may be able to make more of all this than we can. In any case you'll have to keep your eyes open a lot more. I don't like this story about a disappearing note. As we suspected, there must be people in on this thing that we don't know about. You're quite sure, are you, that this dope did write something and put it in the letterbox?'

'I'm fed up with this!' grumbled Paul. 'How many times do I have to tell you? All right, once more: when the old dear next door told Maillard Bernard must be away, he went to the light and wrote something on a page of his notebook. Then he went back towards Bernard's house, and though I couldn't see exactly what he was doing he must have put the paper through the letterbox on the gate. Later on, when I'd tied him up and brought him back here, I went over to swipe the note, but there was nothing either in the box or on the ground.'

'Had you been away long?'

'Quite a while. After I'd knocked Maillard out I had to hide in a ditch with him until that army convoy had gone by. I'd have been a bit conspicuous with two bicycles and a limp body. I came back by a longer way, across the waste ground, and had to make a second trip to get the bikes, so that took up some more time.'

'You didn't see anyone?'

'No. Somebody must have snaffled the note while I was lying in the mud.'

Dédé swore. 'Hell! not only is there a stranger nosing around but we don't even know what was in the note he took . . . But listen, Paul, I've had a thought: he wrote his message in a notebook, didn't he? . . . It must have been the one you showed me, since you say that was all he had on him besides the wallet. No pen or pencil? Or perhaps you took them? Like you did his cash?'

'No. No pen or pencil.'

'It must have fallen out when he came off his bike. There's just a chance . . . Let's have a look.' I could hear Dédé turning the pages, exclaiming from time to time: 'Yes . . . here we are . . . no . . . just a minute . . .', then, triumphantly: 'Here it is!' He explained to Paul that on the other side of the page on which Maillard had scribbled his note there was one of the drawings they'd mentioned earlier, executed with a soft pencil. It had functioned like carbon paper, leaving a faint second copy of the original note on the next page. The two pored over the notebook trying to decipher the words. They managed to make out '*husband . . . came to see . . . Lynx*'.

'It doesn't make sense!' said Paul.

'It's a code,' explained Dédé knowingly, but he was obviously disappointed.

'Lynx . . . there were a lot of magazines called *The Lynx* in his flat.'

'Yeah, it's a detective story weekly. But the explanation's bound to be something more subtle than that.'

They pondered for a while. It was Dédé who broke the silence. 'We'll leave it for the moment. I'm no good at guessing games – that sort of thing's more in Jackie's line. What we've got to do is get rid of this stiff.'

'You're right there,' agreed Paul. 'I can't be doing

with him around for long – it may be cold but soon he'll start to make his presence smelt.'

'What do you plan to do with him?'

'Wait until it gets dark and then go and chuck him down a well I noticed about a hundred yards from here. It's dried up and no one goes there. Also there are rats. And no one'll notice an extra pong – there's a terrible smell round here already.'

'There certainly is! Sooner you than me! Don't worry, Paul, you won't have to stew here much longer. Jackie'll be back and she'll sort things out.'

They decided that although there was probably no point, the watch on the house across the road had better go on or it'd give Jackie something else to grouse about. They hoped she'd had better luck than they had. Then Paul saw Dédé to the side door, telling him to make a detour round the old woman's house – she might be deaf but she wasn't blind! – and came grumbling back up to the room where the body was.

I waited long enough for Dédé to get out of earshot, for I had a feeling things were soon going to get a bit lively between Paul and me. I could hear him muttering away in the next room and keeping up his spirits with swigs of red wine. He might be handy at bumping people off but he was no good at guarding their corpses. And he was making me feel thirsty. He needed teaching a lesson.

I suddenly burst out of my cupboard and leapt into the next room. At the sound of the creaking door, Paul swung round gaping with astonishment. Grasping my trusty pipe I pointed it, still in my pocket, at the gangster. 'Hands up, Paul!' I shouted.

He wasn't quite so dim as I'd thought, and it didn't take him long to work out that invisible guns aren't always what they're made out to be. Also that, in 1942, with the clothing shortage, I wasn't likely to shoot through the pocket of a perfectly good coat. But I wasn't just paying a friendly call either. He didn't hesitate.

His hand had moved so fast it was just a dark blur. Then I was facing a hail of random bullets. But if he was quick, I was quicker. I flung myself down flat and the bullets tore past me into the wall, spraying the room with plaster. I jumped to my feet. What luck! Maillard was a mere featherweight: I propped up the body and used it as a shield — I could hear the dull thud as the bullets rained into it. Then I gave it a violent shove towards Paul. Horrified and taken off balance, he was toppled by its weight and fell to the floor, dropping his shooter.

I sprang on top of him and we struggled fiercely, our flailing arms and legs hampered by the unfortunate corpse. What with one thing and another, if a police pathologist ever got hold of him he was going to think he'd fallen under a train.

Paul had recovered himself and was trying to retrieve the gun, but I managed to kick it away across the room. It teetered on the edge of one of the numerous holes in the floor, then slowly toppled through. We heard it land on the kitchen floor. Mad with rage, Paul started hitting out wildly, and as I returned his blows I edged round towards the corner he used as a larder. Grabbing a bottle of red wine I crashed it down on his head with all my might.

Wine streamed through his hair and down on to his face and shirt. There must have been blood mixed with it, but I can't say it bothered me. With a little groan, he folded up like an accordion and sank senseless to the floor. As there was clearly nothing to be got out of him for the moment, I tied his ankles together with the scarf and handkerchief. I was just undoing the cords on Maillard's wrists to transfer them to his killer when I heard a sound outside like pebbles crunching underfoot. Squinting through the boards on the window, I looked across towards B-B-B's house. A man was standing in the middle of the road staring towards the spot where I stood watching. He looked puzzled and hesitant. I'd seen his face on one of the photos on the old woman's sideboard. His right hand was freshly bandaged. He must have had an accident at work that morning and come home early.

While Paul and I fondly imagined there was no one about to overhear our high jinks, he'd been there all the time, and now had come out to investigate the sound of gunshots.

'This won't do, Nestor my lad,' I thought. 'He'll be off to call the police before you can say knife.' And in fact, after going briefly back indoors, he emerged again and set off in the direction of the town. It was time for me to scarper if I didn't want to find myself carrying the can for Paul. He was still out for the count. I gave him a kick or two, but he didn't stir. A pity – I'd have liked to take him with me. And have something to show for my trouble.

I went through his pockets and removed everything, including the money – it could go towards my fare!

I left the two sleeping beauties to it, and, without even pausing in the kitchen to pick the revolver up off the floor, went and collected my bike from the old woman's shed. No one was around. I set off for the sweet factory, pedalling as fast as I could go.

11 The man who killed Nestor Burma

'My word,' giggled Rouget when he saw me. 'What've you been doing, making love to a female cannonball?'

'Something like that,' I answered. 'Could you lend me a clothes-brush?'

He produced one, remarking that if I wanted to be smuggled over the line a needle and thread wouldn't come amiss either, otherwise I'd draw attention to the whole party.

'I've put off my departure,' I told him while I tidied up myself as best I could. 'I'm needed here in Marseilles.'

'What! After I've sweated my guts out . . . '

'I must send an interzone card to Hélène,' I cut in, 'but I don't want it posted from here.'

'Careful as ever!'

'*More* than ever. Can't you detect a whiff of dead bodies in the air?'

'It's been like that since 1939.'

'I'm not talking about the war. Listen, do you know anyone in Cannes or Perpignan or somewhere who could post a card for me?'

He knew someone in Nice.

When I came back from posting off the card with a covering note, I retired to my mattress among the dried fruit and went through the things I'd taken from the unconscious Paul. Identity and ration cards told me he was Paul Clément, born at Cahors in 1909 and now living in Marseilles at 33C Angel Passage. There were two sets of keys, one of them Maillard's, also Maillard's papers and the notebook that had puzzled Dédé and Paul so much.

The money, including what Paul had taken from Maillard, totalled three thousand-odd francs – better than nothing. I'd be able to buy a respectable raincoat to replace the old one, which hadn't been the same since the fight.

I lit a pipe and lay back on my mattress to think what to do next. I was beginning to realize just what a mess I was in. It sounds very original to be a living corpse, and wanted by the police into the bargain. But having to stay out of sight was cramping my style. I didn't want to put Hélène at risk, or anyone else working for the agency, yet at the moment I could have used two or three assistants. I couldn't be everywhere at once, and there were several visits I needed to pay in a hurry.

First there was the seedy house in the Vieux Port where B-B-B had told me to take the letters. Then I needed to go to Jackie Lamour's place at Cap Croisette. And it was high time I investigated the new guest at the Hôtel Moderne. In fact, that might be the place to start.

At least now I could cross the visit to the late Maillard off the list. I wouldn't be able to discover any more than Paul had, and his description told me enough to be going on with. Perhaps when I had five minutes to spare I'd go round to the Café Riche and check up on a couple of points. As for Paul's place, I didn't intend to go anywhere near it. The police must have nabbed Paul by now, and Angel Passage would be crawling with fuzz. I'd have been walking right into a trap.

After removing a photo of Maillard, I made the rest of Paul's stuff into a bundle and looked for a corner to hide it in while Rouget wasn't looking. He was a good bloke, and obliging enough, but it was better if he didn't know he was harbouring a powder keg with the fuse lit.

The hiding-place I found was already in use. It contained a gun of Spanish make, large enough to be used as a cosh if the ammunition ran out. It was practically fully loaded and seemed to be in good working order. Just what I needed. And now I was armed to the teeth, I might as well keep Paul's stuff with me.

Leaving Rouget's amazing factory, I set off to look for Marc Covet. If he was in Marseilles he might be useful. At the office of one of the local rags I asked to speak to Lagarde. I knew from that day's issue he was in charge of the local news items, not a very thrilling collection in these days of censorship. The rule seemed to be 'No violent deaths, please, there's a war on.'

I found Lagarde sitting at his desk, contemplating the ample curves of an insipid-looking typist. He was doubtless thinking how in more carefree times he could have dismembered her to make some juicy copy. As I went in, he tore his eyes away and turned his stubbly chops enquiringly in my direction.

I put on an ingratiating smile. 'I'm Martin,' I said. 'I'm looking for a colleague of yours from Paris – Marc Covet, of the *Crépuscule*.'

'I've heard the name.'

'Do you know if he's in Marseilles?'

'What do you think this is, an information desk?'

'OK, OK. But you newspaper boys always know what's going on, don't you? Am I right in thinking some of your chums who write for the Paris papers have turned up in Marseilles recently?'

'Write for the Germans, you mean! They're no chums of mine.'

'So they *are* here. Do you know where they hang out? I was thinking of lobbing a bomb at them.'

He looked me up and down. 'A terrorist, are you? You don't look like one.' He ought to have known the number of corpses I'd met in the last few days! 'I'm just a beginner,' I said.

'All right,' he said, with a laugh. 'You'll find the chaps you're after at the Moderne. But hurry up with your bomb – they're leaving soon.'

We parted with expressions of mutual esteem. I was pleased with what I'd learned: Marc Covet at the Moderne, too – what could be handier?

Covet was still in bed. It was midday, but he wasn't bothered. It looked as if he'd had a few the night before. He still had his shirt and tie on.

'Oh, you're still around,' he said. 'Not been shot yet?'

'Give it time,' I answered, parking myself on the bed. 'There are four bodies in the case already.'

'And you're inviting me to be the fifth?'

'Come on, be serious. I've got a job for you. It'll make a great story for you after the war. If you only knew, you'd be hiring staff already to type it up. It's gripping stuff. Go and stick your head under the tap and I'll tell you all about it.'

'Get off my feet then.' He rolled out of bed. He'd been sleeping in his socks and pants. Now he was having problems standing up straight.

'Been on the town, eh?'

'We never left the hotel!' he protested.

'You can go on the town inside a hotel. I should know.'

'That's what we did,' he said, pulling a face.

I could hear him splashing about and grumbling in the bathroom. 'Going back to Paris, aren't we? Got to make the most of our expense accounts, haven't we? So we were in the bar from seven last night right through to seven this morning.'

He came back, mopping his face with a towel. He looked a bit more on the ball.

'In the bar, eh?' I said. 'In that case, did you see anyone check in during the night?'

The artful look that came into his eye encouraged me. He said, 'Perhaps you should buy me a hair of the dog. Pastis is good for hangovers. And it's very good for the memory.'

'Call room service then . . . So you did notice something going on?'

As we downed two of room service's specials I asked him to tell me about the new arrivals.

'There was only one,' he said, 'though he caused as much commotion as if there'd been three of him. I happened to call at reception for something or other and there he was, filling in his registration form. Great red beefy face, enough to make you throw up. He looked like a German to me, but I couldn't swear to it.'

'What was all the fuss about? Did he have a lot of luggage?'

'No, only the one case. But he asked for pen and paper and wrote a note that he said had to be delivered pronto. The staff were livid. They're a lazy lot – must be the climate down here. Or maybe the tip wasn't enough. Anyway, he went up to his room, but he didn't go to bed straight away. I saw him in the lounge a couple of hours later when I went out there for a breather.'

'It sounds like the man I'm looking for,' I said. 'Listen, Marc. Will you do something for me? It's not what I came for, but what you've just said changes things. I want you to tell me exactly what this man looked like. Then I want you to find out his room number, where he sent that message, whether he made or received any phone calls. I need to know his name – or at any rate the one he gave – and what he was up to in the lounge two hours after he got here.'

'Will that be all?' enquired Covet ironically.

'It'll do to be going on with. I'll have one or two more little errands for you later.'

'Oh good. I *am* glad. Well, it's your turn now.'

'What do you mean, my turn?'

'To do something for me. You promised to tell me all about the case.'

As I needed to get him interested, I did tell him most of it. He'd never heard of Victor Fernèse, but he was very shocked by what'd happened to Frédéric Delan. He went on for a while about what a terrible thing it was. Then – life must go on – he looked at his watch and suggested that as he wasn't much of a hand at descriptions we should go down to the hotel dining-room to see if we could get a look at the new guest. That was *his* story. It was as good an excuse as any to cadge a free lunch off me.

We sat down at a corner table with a view of the whole room, and soon Covet pointed out the man I was interested in. Apart from the brick-red face, he wasn't a very noticeable figure as he sat there concentrating on his food and his glass of beer. He looked peaceable, almost bovine. He had fair hair, plastered to his scalp, and a tiny moustache. His well-cut neutral-coloured suit was of pre-war quality.

He took a pull at his drink, set down the glass and looked casually round the room. Casually? The piercing blue eyes were colder than ice, and in spite of his quiet manner I could sense the underlying inflexibility. Suddenly I knew I'd seen this man before . . . dressed differently, and with glasses. It was Otto Whatsisname – the Pink Potato – the one who'd tried to arrest me – the one who'd thought up the idea of saying I was dead! In other words – my murderer.

We didn't linger over the rest of our meal. I didn't want the German cop to recognize me, assuming he hadn't already done so – it was impossible to tell from his manner. Once we were back in the journalist's room I explained what I wanted him to do. Since he had a working relationship with the police I'd have liked him to ask what they'd made of the Maillard business and the part played in it by Paul, who must be in jug by now. But that would have to wait.

'I want you to keep a close watch on the man we saw downstairs,' I told Marc. 'If he goes out, follow him. I'll give you the phone number of Allfruit in case of emergencies. I may be there to answer, I may not. If not, use your discretion. It's not much of a system, but it's the best I can manage for now. No need to pull a face! I told you – I'm letting you in on a case that'll make you famous once there's a free press again.'

'How do you make that out?' he asked. 'As far as I can see, this is just like all the other cases we've been in together, except that this one's more dangerous, with Germans thrown in.'

'Ah, but you're forgetting the letters! Even after reading them I don't know exactly what's in them, but with all those people running after them they must have something other letters haven't got.'

'All right,' he agreed, 'but unless we can lay hands on them, what good are they going to do us? You don't happen to have them on you, I suppose?'

I smiled at his sarcasm and he gave me a suspicious look.

'You're holding out on me!' he said accusingly.

I had to admit that I was. 'There's something I can't tell you because I don't even like to think about it myself. It's something I can only tell to – well, to a priest.'

'To a what?' he spluttered. 'But why?'

'Because he'd be too polite to say I was barmy.'

'Maybe he would. I wouldn't. And I should know after all this time. Anyhow, I'm off downstairs to see what our man's up to.' He was raring to go. My patter had had the desired effect.

I walked along the Canebière to the Vieux Port. German soldiers, watched curiously by the local people, came and went along the waterfront. I reached the street where the house I'd been summoned to by B-B-B stood.

Only it didn't. There was a great hole in the blackened façade, and sky showed through the gaping windows. The 'Japanese' room was being aired for the first time. The houses on either side were damaged too, but not to the same extent. It must have been here that the German officer was shot and reprisals were taken. This was bad news for my investigation. I didn't try to question the neighbours, a couple of flabby-looking pros who didn't look anxious to talk.

I went back to the factory to fetch my bike, then set off for Cap Croisette. I was almost sure I wouldn't find anything at Jackie Lamour's, but I had to know for certain.

The weather was fine again. I rode along the coast in a pleasant breeze. Pale sunlight warmed the shimmering sea. I thought how much hotter, in every sense of the word, it must be on the other side of the water.

I came to the top of a hill and, looking down through the pines at the villa, decided not to approach it by the normal route, the turning off the main road. I had to be careful. If the dancer was at home she might see me on the road. I went on until I reached a little wood behind the house. Leaving my bike there, I continued on foot across some rough ground where tamarisk bushes and scrub hid me from view. When I saw that the shutters at the windows were open, I gave myself a mental pat on the back for being so careful. Unless Jackie had moved out for good and other tenants moved in, which didn't seem likely, either she must have got back from her expedition to the Occupied Zone or I'd find some of her sidekicks in there.

I chucked a stone at one of the window-panes. The racket it made as it shattered was tremendous. I waited, crouching out of sight among the bushes, but no one appeared at any of the windows. Good – for the moment I had the place to myself. I got up and ran to the door, the one whose lock I'd smashed the time I'd wanted her to think she'd had burglars. Now the lock had been repaired and the door was shut fast. But I got it open without much difficulty.

Inside, I wondered what to do. What exactly was I hoping to find here? Nothing, really: I wanted to soak up the atmosphere, to find clues to heaven knew what in heaven knew which insignificant detail. That had been my original motive for coming. Now that I knew by the open shutters that the house hadn't been empty while the dancer was away, I had something more to look forward to: the arrival, any minute now, of the current occupant. Another Dédé, maybe?

A dark corridor brought me to the sitting-room. It was flooded with bright sunlight, and looked pretty much as I had seen it the evening of the brawl. But one thing was different. I could swear someone had been ferreting around. There was nothing to see: it was more something you felt. And there was something else, something equally hard to put your finger on. No one was actually living here: those shutters had only just been opened. No one was actually living here . . . but . . . Yes, there must be someone around.

As I stood thinking, in the middle of the sitting-room and facing the window, I suddenly had the distinct impression there was someone else present. So distinct I didn't bother to reach for my revolver. I knew it would be useless: there was already a gun trained on my back.

I spun round.

A man was leaning in the doorway. Everything about him looked sardonic, even his moustache. Under the brim of his brown felt hat his gaze was mocking. I was right: he was holding a revolver. But more for decoration than anything else.

What a relief! With all the excitement, I'd almost forgotten that my old friend was also coming down to the coast.

'Hallo there!' I smiled. 'How's tricks, Florimond?'

12 Light is shed

The policeman put his gun away. 'What the devil are you doing here, Burma?' he snapped.

'That's no way to speak to a ghost,' I protested. 'Anyway, don't you know spirits always return to the scene of the crime?'

'Ghost you may be, but you and I are going to have a little chat. And no nonsense, d'you understand?'

He called 'Down here!' to someone I couldn't see. I heard footsteps overhead, and soon we were joined by two men, one massive and pale, the other thin and swarthy. Both looked like cops, probably because they were.

'Gentlemen,' said Faroux, 'this is Dynamite Burma, whom you've heard so much about. Nestor, my lad, this' – pointing to the dark one – 'is Bonvalet, from the local police. And that's Inspector Grégoire, one of my men from Paris. You must know him by sight. He's down here with me to find out why the Germans are so bothered about the murder of Sdenko Matich.'

'Delighted to meet you, gentlemen. What a good hostess you make, Florimond.'

The Superintendent wasn't amused. 'Stop fooling about, Burma! I suppose you're going to tell me you're just here by chance. Looking for a house to rent, or hunting butterflies, or some such rubbish. Well, it won't wash. When the Croat was done in you were in the same train. You'd both come from Marseilles. You were more or less alike to look at. Now I find you in the house of a woman we know had dealings with Matich.'

'Oh, so they were acquainted, were they?'

He made a gesture of impatience. 'As if you didn't know! Now I'll be plain with you. I'm here on an unofficial mission.' And he started to talk of patriotism, higher interests, sacred duty. Very edifying.

Suddenly he changed tack. 'And I shan't let scruples stand in my way,' he said. 'The situation's too serious. I'm completely stymied and I think you're the only one who can help me out. So you'd better talk of your own free will, or else . . . '

'Talking's thirsty work,' I objected. 'What have you got to drink?'

'If we look round, I daresay we might hit . . . on something,' said Grégoire, with a meaning look.

'Did you know the Germans are looking for you?' asked Faroux.

I didn't answer at once. After a moment's reflection, 'I think we ought to come to some arrangement,' I said. 'You're making a song and dance about what I know or don't know. But the joke is, when I've told you, you'll realize you already knew it.'

'Try me.'

'Just a minute. You say you're interested in this case. Well, so am I.'

'But why? That's one of the things I want to find out.'

'For sentimental reasons,' I explained. 'You needn't smirk – it's true. At first I thought I was the one they meant to kill, not the Croat. I came down here for a word with the owner of the finger I thought was on the trigger. But he was dead, too . . . Someone had beaten me to it. Then someone else bowed out, and I feel responsible for his death. His name was Maillard – you must have found his body at Saint-Barnabé when your men went to pull in Paul Clément. Maybe it's because revenge is in the air, but I feel strongly about avenging this bloke's death.'

Grégoire and Bonvalet cleared their throats. Florimond Faroux struck his palm with his fist. 'I knew you had something worth listening to, Burma,' he exclaimed. 'I knew it as soon as I saw you creep out of the bushes. I said as much to the others. By the way, you were a bit too clever this time. Coming up from behind, you missed seeing our car.'

'On the contrary, my caution paid off. If I'd seen the car I might have just gone away. Whereas now I'm very glad we've met . . . I get the impression,' I continued, 'that the names Maillard and Clément are completely new to you, and you don't know what happened at Saint-Barnabé. I thought someone had gone to call the police, but he must have changed his mind and kept it all to himself. These southerners! If I'd realized, I'd have hung on there to keep an eye on Clément. Then I might have found out a bit more.'

'You're already a mine of information.'

'Maybe. But I expect some from you in exchange – you didn't come here to admire the scenery. Fair's fair, Florimond. Let's pool what we know, and we might shed a bit of daylight on this case. It's very involved, you can take it from me.'

'Are your cases ever anything but? Anyway – from now on we cooperate. Carry on then, Burma, we're listening.'

So I started to tell my story. Parts of it. I recalled

how I'd been paid thirty thousand francs, how I'd come here a few nights back to burgle Jackie Lamour, and so on. I didn't tell them the Pink Potato was in Marseilles, nor give the name or description of Dédé, Paul Clément's accomplice. I was hoping to get to Dédé through the German, and then pump some information out of him about the letters. This was a personal matter and I didn't want Faroux interfering. I also left out the tragic interlude at the mental home. There were enough complications already, and I didn't think the superintendent would be much help to me there. I could tell him about Delan's death later on, when things had been sorted out a bit.

'And what do you think it all means?' asked Faroux when I'd concluded my edited version of events.

'Let me get my breath back, will you! And meanwhile you can tell me what point your own enquiries have reached.'

'Oh, us!' he said, ironically. 'We had a photograph of the Croat and a few other details. So we've been trying to find out what he was doing in Marseilles. We discovered that he had dealings with Jackie Lamour, and we came to see if we could pick up something in her house. That's all.'

'And what did you find?'

'Nothing!' said Inspector Grégoire, not concealing his annoyance. 'But the padlocks on the windows looked suspicious.'

'You know now why they were there. Did all the windows have padlocks on them?'

'Yes, but they weren't all fastened.'

'Once the letters were gone there was no point,' I said.

'Everything comes back to those blasted letters,' said Faroux. 'We need to know what their real message is, and we need to get hold of them. It's not going to be easy.'

'Especially if I'm right in thinking they may no longer exist.'

The superintendent's eyes widened. 'What do you mean?'

'Just a hunch. M. Bonvalet can tell me whether there's anything in it.'

The local cop gave me a puzzled look. 'That house in the Vieux Port,' I explained, 'the one where B-B-B and I met for the last time. It's the only place where there's been any trouble since the German troops arrived in town. It may not be a coincidence. Do you know anything about that house, M. Bonvalet?'

'There's a rumour that it's a staging post for people escaping to Algeria. The Germans knew, and they sent a Gestapo officer with a tank crew to attack the place. But the people inside didn't wait around to be shot at – they fired first, and killed the officer. The tank then shelled the house, but some of the people got away and still haven't been found.'

'Well,' I suggested, 'perhaps the North African landing had put a stop to the smuggling of refugees. Perhaps B-B-B had been intending to go over to Algeria with the letters, and that was why he looked so upset the second time I saw him. Perhaps while he was waiting for things to get back to normal he left the letters somewhere in the house. Perhaps with the madam . . . That may be why he didn't want me to leave at the same time as he did – he wanted to talk to her . . . What's become of her, by the way?'

'She was killed in the shooting,' said Grégoire.

'The letters must have gone up in flames at the same time as the house,' I went on. 'B-B-B couldn't have kept them, otherwise Jackie's little pals would have found them at his place at the time of the torture incident, and not needed to watch the house . . . Good grief!'

'What?' asked Faroux suspiciously.

'It's this rotten pipe – it doesn't draw properly,' I lied, taking the blameless object out of my mouth and pretending to examine the stem. In fact I'd just had an idea that might explain what the kidnapping of Victor Fernèse was all about.

'By the way,' said Faroux, 'who is this Maillard character?'

'He's just an innocent victim with a thing about who-dunnits – he had a complete collection of *The Lynx* in his flat. No way was he Bernard's accomplice – he met him exactly as he told me. M. Bonvalet will no doubt be checking on that. When B-B-B heard Maillard was going to be away, he seized the opportunity of borrowing his flat to interview me in.

'Maillard no doubt assumed he was going to use it as a love-nest. When I called, he saw my ring and thought I must be the deceived husband. He was delighted to have a part to play in the drama, and rushed off to put Bernard on his guard. When he got to Saint–Barnabé he found nobody in, so in true shilling-shocker style he left a note signed, 'The Lynx'. From then on, the poor devil had a real rôle in a real crime story. He was going to play the corpse, and it was all my fault.'

'My heart bleeds,' said Faroux.

'You can laugh,' I said, 'but I feel terrible about it. That man's death is on my conscience, and avenging it is a matter of honour.'

'Is that why you're so determined to go on with the case?'

'Yes, it is. At first it was the letters I was interested in, but now I think we can kiss them goodbye.'

'Yeah,' agreed the superintendent, stroking his moustache. 'Still, whether the letters have been destroyed or not, the dancing-girl's gang are still on the loose.'

'And perhaps there's something else besides the letters,' ventured Inspector Grégoire.

'If there is, I'm damn well going to find out,' growled Faroux. 'Let's get on with it. You've given us some useful clues, Burma. I was starting to think it was hopeless, with the girl gone and no leads.'

He went on: 'We'll start by having Bernard's body brought in and finding out what we can about his past. Then we'll search Paul Clément's place. Maillard will have to be investigated too. You've suggested one explanation for his actions, but there may be another.'

'You'd have to investigate Maillard anyway to check my theory, so carry on,' I said. 'But I don't think there's any point in going to Clément's house. He's probably flown the coop by now. You've seen what he had in his pockets – he's not the type to have written his memoirs. He can't have left anything more informative than the furniture.'

'Angel Passage is full of gossiping old women,' put in Bonvalet. 'If Clément had any visitors, we'll be told. And a character like that's probably got a police record too.'

'Has Jackie Lamour got one?' I inquired. 'She's certainly up to something, that chick – apart from flaunting herself in night-clubs. And surely Jackie Lamour can't be her real name?'

'No, it's Jacqueline Barre,' said Faroux.

'Her middle name's not Laurence, by any chance?' I interrupted.

'No. Why?'

'It doesn't matter. Go on.'

He threw me a dubious glance, but went on.

'She came to live in Marseilles not long after the armistice, in July 1940. She's a professional dancer and has worked in France and abroad. She was in trouble with the law at one time over currency dealings. She has very mixed connections and is known to be very peculiar.'

'And,' I added, 'she's got the mark of a bullet wound on one arm. Not exactly an innocent maiden, eh? What about the Croat?'

'When he was here he stayed in a hotel where they're not over-strict about registration. He said he'd come from Nice, but we've found out it wasn't true. And another thing: it wasn't his first visit to Marseilles. He was here for a short time two months ago, and stayed in the same hotel.'

'Did he see Jackie Lamour on that occasion?'

'Difficult to say. We're making inquiries.'

'Any connection with the Croatian terrorists?'

'Definitely not. When King Alexander was assassinated, Matich wasn't in France.'

'But the letters are signed "Petrus", which is the Christian name of Kalemen, the killer of Karageorgevich.'

'So what?' said Faroux. 'According to you the letters are all love stuff. You think they're really about something else?'

'Yes, I do,' I replied.

'Petrus . . . Petrus . . . ' mused the Superintendent, looking intense. His moustache bristled. 'You're sure it was Petrus?'

'Well, not exactly Petrus, just the first four letters. P,e,t,r . . . It could only be short for Petrus or Petronella, as far as I can see.'

Faroux exchanged a rapid glance with his men, triumph glinting in his eyes. 'How about "Petroleum"?', he suggested.

It's only right the official police should occasionally be the ones to solve mysteries. That's what they're paid for. But I couldn't help feeling a bit of a fool. And yet . . .

'My God!' I exclaimed after a moment. 'The black ribbon!'

'Black ribbon?'

'The one tied round the letters. I didn't understand what it stood for before. Oil – black gold – black ribbon. Instead of wasting time over "Peter" or "Petrus", I ought to have spotted at once that it stood for "Petroleum".'

'I expect it's because you're only used to complicated cases,' mocked Faroux. 'Never mind – you'd have thought of "Petroleum" before I did if you'd known what I knew about Matich.'

'What did you know?'

'You remember our conversation in Paris, when I said Matich was some sort of expert in oil? Well, when I got down here I just happened to take on Bonvalet as my assistant. He was stationed in Toulouse before the war and remembered having Matich under surveillance as an immigrant worker. At that time Matich had a job on the oil well at Saint-Gaudens, about a hundred kilometres from Toulouse.'

'But when war broke out he suddenly vanished,' interposed Bonvalet. 'Up till then he hadn't a stain on his character. But it's no surprise to find him mixed up with mysterious letters signed "Petr" – or Petroleum.'

At the name Saint-Gaudens my heart had turned over. I affected a composure I was far from feeling as I summed up: 'So you conclude the letters are something to do with oil. Well, I've read them, and if that's what the message is, it's far from obvious!'

'There must be some sort of a code.'

'Yes, but even if we had the key it wouldn't do us any good. Because the letters were hidden in the house in the Vieux Port – I'm sure of it – and they went up in smoke with the building.'

'Whether you're right or wrong, I'm going on with my inquiries,' declared Faroux. 'We're going to investigate Bernard, Maillard and Clément, and as we go along we may find some clues that'll help us put a spoke in the Germans' wheel. Since they're taking an interest in the killing of the Croat, it's our duty to get to the bottom of it ourselves.'

'I wonder,' I said, 'why you ever let yourself in for all this trouble?'

'Why did *you?*'

'Oh, I like adventure.'

'And I've got my orders.' He turned to his men. 'Now, let's get going. Put everything back where it was, close the shutters, and we'll be off. Burma, if you want a lift back, go and get your bike and we'll tie it to the side of the car.'

13 Formula 5

When I got back to Allfruit the people there seemed to be in as agitated a state as I was.

'What's going on?' I inquired.

'We've been searched again,' Rouget told me. 'We were getting used to the French cops doing it, but just now it was the Germans. If they keep on it's going to be dangerous for the Jews we shelter. Anyway the Jerries had calmed down, luckily, by the time they left. When they arrived they were livid – they must have been told we were hiding something or other on the premises. But when they didn't find it and we put on our air of injured innocence they went away thinking we were the victims of slander. But we're going to have to be more careful.'

'I hope it wasn't me they were looking for,' I said.

'They didn't say.'

'I'm glad I wasn't here, anyway!' When I'd recovered from my retrospective fright I asked Rouget whether by any chance he had an oil specialist among his 'political' protégés, if possible a person with some high-powered gen on the subject that I could have a look at.

Rouget looked dubious. 'The chaps who come here don't have time to bring their books with them,' he said. 'But I think I can fix you up. There's a schoolmaster in the town who lost his job because of his political activities, though he's not a militant now. He once published a paper on oil and he's got all the current documentation. He should be able to come up with what you want. Are you writing an article too?'

'You have to do something to pass the time, don't you? The name, please?'

'Marius Alicot – lives in the rue Félix Pyat.'

'Right then, I'm off to see him. No phone calls for me while I was away?' There were none, so I rang the Moderne. Covet wasn't there.

Comrade Alicot looked like a bookworm. He was well into his fifties, with an amiable manner, a goatee and an ample moustache stained with nicotine. Behind steel-rimmed glasses bright blue eyes gleamed with mischief. He lived in a little two-roomed flat filled to bursting with books, pamphlets, periodicals and piles of newspapers of all descriptions. I mentioned Jean Rouget's name and explained the object of my visit.

'Have a seat.' He shoved a heap of papers off a decrepit armchair. 'There are five hundred or more books here on oil technology. Help yourself – you can take all night over it if you want to.'

'Before I start I'd like if I may to ask a question – your answer could save me a lot of trouble.'

'I'm at your service. Ask away!'

'What does the word "formula" mean to you, in connection with oil? It probably sounds mad,' I went on, seeing his air of astonishment, 'but I've only the one word to go on. I need to know what it refers to, and it looks as though I'm going to have to plough through all these books to find out.'

'Formula? Formula for what?'

'That's just what I don't know!'

'What made you come to me then?'

'The formula I'm talking about is one of a series: "Formula 5" is a phrase I heard used by someone who used to work as an engineer in the Saint-Gaudens field. You may know him – before he went out of his mind, poor fellow, he was a militant pacifist, so your paths may have crossed. His name's Victor Fernèse.' And I told him as much as I could of the man's history.

M. Alicot shook his head. 'I haven't been a member of a political organization for nearly twenty years,' he said. 'Victor Fernèse? No, the name means absolutely nothing to me, I'm afraid.'

'And "Formula 5"?'

'You said the man who used the phrase was mad, didn't you?' he smiled.

'Yes – mad as a hatter. But I'm certain the words make sense.'

'You may be right. Myself, I can't see what they refer to.'

'Oh, well,' I sighed, 'it can't be helped. I'd better make a start on the books. That cursed phrase may occur in one of them.'

'Good luck then!'

He led me to the relevant shelves, and while I settled down with my pipe and an armful of yellowed tomes he stood beside me and refreshed his memory by leafing through some articles on his favourite subject.

I'd still made no progress when my host uttered a sudden exclamation. 'Good God! My memory's not what it used to be! "Formula 5" – that should have rung a bell at once!'

'Have you had an idea?' I asked eagerly.

'I think so. Could "Formula 5" have something to do with drilling or extraction?'

'It might.'

'Listen,' said Alicot, tapping the volume he was holding and producing a puff of dust. 'There's a paragraph here that should solve your problem. I could kick myself for not thinking of it straight away. If your "Formula 5" really exists outside the fevered imagination of a madman, it's something of enormous importance. And I'm speaking as an expert.'

I asked him to explain.

'Well, now . . . ' He sat down on a rickety stool. I was quivering with impatience. 'At present there are only four known methods for detecting, drilling, and extracting oil. The first is very rudimentary and hasn't been used since about 1882. Three other methods have been invented since, each in some respect an improvement on the one before, either because it leads to greater efficiency in detection or drilling, or because it allows a higher percentage of the petroleum to be extracted. For example, did you know this . . . ' Following the text with his finger he read aloud:

In the present state of technology total extraction of oil deposits
is not practicable . . . As existing wells become depleted,
the cartels are prospecting worldwide in an attempt to locate
potential reserves with which to cater for increased
consumption. These operations are very expensive. The failure
rate is 70 per cent.*

He stopped and looked at me. Although his stove was giving off more noxious fumes than heat, I was sweating with tension.

* Le Pétrole et la Guerre (Oil and War), by Raymond Dior.

'Do you think it feasible that a petro-engineer might invent a "Formula 5" that would overcome the problem of drilling failures and incomplete extraction?'

'Anything called "Formula 5" could only refer to that. However,' he added, 'remember we're discussing the words of a madman.'

'Madman be damned!' I cried. 'He hadn't always been mad, and there are plenty of sane people interested in what he said. The awful truth is that Formula 5 is a reality.'

Alicot shot me a curious look as he drew on the cigarette protruding from among his whiskers.

'What do you mean?'

'Only that Formula 5 exists, and that it too represents an advance on its predecessors. I haven't any proof, but suppose I'm right: do you think it could upset the oil market and affect the fuel crisis?'

'Certainly.'

'Could there be people who'd stop at nothing to get hold of the secret?'

The former schoolmaster gave a sardonic laugh. 'According to Clemenceau, a drop of oil is worth a drop of blood. You can take that whichever way you like.'

'True enough: oil and blood go together . . . It's a strange occupation for a pacifist, though. Unless . . . Could an invention like that prevent wars?'

'Don't make me laugh,' he answered. 'I've got over my youthful illusions.'

'But if you did still have some and you invented a system that ensured successful drilling and complete extraction, wouldn't that make imperialist expansionism unnecessary?'

'Of course,' he said, stroking his beard. 'But it's a big if, and besides having illusions I'd need to be crazy to try.'

'Victor Fernèse did have illusions and he *was* crazy. Later he went completely mad.' I added to myself: 'That was when someone stole the secret on which he'd based an impossible dream of world peace. And in his frenzy he saw as the author and symbol of the theft the man whose name he'd read in all the books about oil: Lawrence of Arabia.'

The case was beginning to take shape.

Fernèse had discovered Formula 5. He had written it down, probably in code, in those letters. At one point they must have been inserted as a precaution amongst some other correspondence, from which they could be distinguished by the signature *Petr*. Then they were stolen (by the Croat? He worked at the same place as the engineer, and could have found out about his research). Anyway, Jackie Lamour got hold of them later on, and it was certainly the Croat she got them from. I pinched them off her for B-B-B, who in response to a little gentle persuasion revealed that they were still in the house in the Vieux Port. That didn't help her much because the house had been destroyed. It was then, when she was at her wits' end, that she went and snatched Fernèse from the mental home where he was a patient, hoping to take advantage of one of his lucid moments to force his secret out of him. There was no time to lose now since, as was clear from the conversation I overheard between Dédé and Paul, a customer was already on his way to take delivery of the documents. Was this customer the Pink Potato? It could be him, or it could be someone else, but in any case the Pink Potato was in Marseilles, and his lot were specialists in coded messages.

This analysis had some gaps and some assumptions in it, but I trusted my intuition and felt I wasn't far out. I was quite pleased with myself. I was several steps ahead of Jackie, though there was still a lot of tough work in front of me. And the next thing to do was . . . nothing! For the moment there was no alternative: I just had to wait for things to happen. But I was getting edgy.

I stayed on a bit, discussing my hypothesis about Formula 5 with Alicot in order to convince myself there was something in it. Then, as it was getting late, I took my leave of my obliging host and made my way back to the sweet factory, hoping to find a message from Marc Covet waiting for me. There wasn't one. I rang the Moderne and he came to the phone. Nothing of interest to report, but if I cared to go round there in the morning he'd tell me more and we could have a drink together. From this I gathered that Rote-Kartoffel, alias the Pink Potato, was somewhere in the neighbourhood of the phone booth, which might not be completely soundproof, and that Marc hadn't lost the trail. That was something anyway. I said I'd see him in the morning and hung up.

The mention of drinks had made me thirsty, but when I got to the nearest bistro I decided I didn't really feel like it. I had a few anyway, to soothe my nerves.

14 Not so good

I slept badly and woke next morning with a hangover which I took with me to my appointment with Marc Covet. Nine o'clock was early for him, but he was already in the hotel lounge flipping through the papers. He looked as bad as I felt, and kept giving cavernous yawns.

'I trust you note my zeal,' he greeted me. 'I've been up since eight ready to follow Korb – that's our man's name – when he comes down.'

'Korb, eh? Well, to me he'll always be the Pink Potato.' I pulled up a chair and sat down.

'If he doesn't go any farther than he did yesterday I can't complain. Tailing him is nothing – the worst part's having to be up and ready at the crack of dawn. Yesterday he only went out late in the afternoon, to take a little constitutional down the Canebière. I don't think he wants to be far from the hotel – he seems to be waiting for something.'

'Whatever it is, don't miss it!'

'I won't!'

'Has he had any visitors?'

'If the bellboy is to be relied on, yes, he has. Yesterday morning, before you were here, a man came asking for him and went straight up to his room.'

'I know about that. Anyone else later?'

'No.'

'Any phone calls in or out?'

'Not that I know of.'

'Any mail?'

'Not a thing.'

'Right. What else?'

'He's in room 109. If you're thinking of searching it . . . '

'I'm not,' I told him. 'I wouldn't find anything. As for talking to him . . . Hm, well . . . I've thought about it, but it's too dangerous.'

'Since when has danger bothered you?'

'This isn't a matter of immediate danger to myself – it's something more general,' I said thoughtfully. 'However . . . Do you know who the note he wrote when he got here was for?'

Covet's face fell. Mine too as he spoke.

'I slipped up badly there,' he admitted. 'The note wasn't delivered by one of the hotel staff, as I assumed. He wrote it at the reception desk all right, but he held on to it. He went to his room, upset the staff by demanding various things they hadn't supplied, and then went out with his letter, to post or deliver it himself. When I saw him later on in the lounge he'd probably just come back. I'd missed that, I'm afraid, when I spoke to you before. My only excuse is that I wasn't supposed to be watching him at that stage. And I was a bit tight, too.'

Bang went my chance to find out where Dédé lived. Unless . . .

'He didn't post the letter, he took it himself,' I said. 'Did he ask anyone in the hotel how to get there?'

'No. Either he knows Marseilles or he asked someone else.'

'The cautious type, eh? He must have known he'd find the person he wanted at home at that time of night, but he wrote them a note just in case.' For a while I puffed in silence at my empty pipe, mourning my lost opportunity and wondering again whether to go up and talk to the man in room 109. I was tempted to do something bold and stupid. But better not: I could afford to wait and see.

'All right, Covet,' I said, rising to go. 'Carry on tailing our man, and keep your eyes open. In the meantime you can buy me a drink, since you insist.'

After spending most of the day trying to contact Florimond Faroux I finally got him on the phone late in the afternoon. Though he knew police premises were not my favourite place, he pressed me to go round and see him at the office he'd been given in the old Bishop's Palace. I found him in a dusty, dimly lit room, attended by the faithful Inspectors Grégoire and Bonvalet. After general handshakes I sat down and asked Faroux what was new.

'We've got more dope on Jackie Lamour. What a vamp, eh? One of our Belgian refugees saw her at the Blackbird Club and recognized her. He told us that three years ago she was living in Brussels with an inventor, until one day she ups and leaves taking his research documents with her. And it wasn't the first time she'd pulled a trick like that, either. So I'm wondering whether she doesn't specialize in stealing industrial secrets. That oil business would fit in nicely.'

Florimond was getting warm!

He continued. 'And Paul Clément, the one who did for Maillard – he's a queer customer too. We didn't find him at Saint-Barnabé, I need hardly say, nor anywhere else.

He had plenty of time after you knocked him out to come to and go off somewhere to hide. But you'd given us his address, so we went and searched his place.'

'And what did you find?'

'Nothing. He'd got there first and removed anything of interest before he scarpered. But this is where police records come in useful. They show that Paul Clément . . . By the way, Bonvalet, what about those further details you chaps were supposed to be getting us?'

The local inspector went to the internal phone and spoke briefly. 'They're on their way,' he announced.

'But you've got some stuff on him already, haven't you?' I said.

'Quite a lot. But Bonvalet can tell it better than I can.'

Bonvalet obediently took up the story. 'Paul Clément has lived in Marseilles long enough to attract the attention of the police. He was mixed up in an unsolved case a while back. The whole thing was pretty unclear, but with what we know now it all falls into place. He had a very minor job in a chemicals factory, and when some documents containing trade secrets went missing he came under suspicion. Nothing could be proved against him and the case fizzled out. But there's no smoke without fire.'

'Well, what do you know!' I exclaimed. 'The lad seems to be in the same line of business as Jackie! Birds of a feather, eh?'

'Exactly,' Faroux agreed.

'My word! you've been busy since yesterday,' I observed. 'No wonder I couldn't get hold of you. Did you find anything on Maillard? Was he interested in secrets too?'

'Sort of: it was mysteries à la Agatha Christie that turned *him* on. He was the victim of his passion for

Hercule Poirot, Arsène Lupin, Inspector Maigret and the rest of the literary super-sleuths. Your theory was right. We found the café he used to go to. The waiters said he sometimes met another customer he'd got to know there – probably through talking about chess problems or crossword puzzles. The other man, of course, was Robert Bernard. The waiters recognized him from our photograph.'

'Was B-B-B a whodunnit fan as well?'

'And how! a real mystery man. Nobody knows where he came from or where he was going or what he lived on. And he wasn't poor either.'

'Far from it: he paid me thirty thousand francs, and he ran a car.'

'Yes, we found it in its usual garage at Saint-Barnabé, but the garage owner didn't know anything. And our search of the house drew a blank too. The post-mortem's today, but . . . ' He shrugged.

'It'll confirm my conjectures,' I said smugly. 'That's something anyway.'

'I'd rather have a lead. There is one, but it's very vague.'

'Is it to do with B-B-B?'

'No, the case as a whole. It's just an idea really, and it probably won't help. Have you ever heard the name Charles Lantenant?'

'It seems to ring a bell.'

'He died in 1937. Used to supply arms to both sides during the Spanish Civil War – and swindled them both as well. His cynicism caught up with him in the end, though. However, it's not his death or his gunrunning that interests me – it's what he did earlier. He'd got up a gang to steal various kinds of secrets and flog them to the highest bidder. I'm wondering whether our friend Jackie hasn't revived the organization.'

'It's quite possible. Where would that leave us?'

'Just where we are now, curse it!'

'So what's your next plan of action?'

'Plan of action!' He laughed bitterly. 'To stay here going round and round in circles until either we all get dizzy and fall down or I'm recalled to Paris. I can't stay here indefinitely, you know – I'm only supposed to be on leave, and one of these days the Germans are going to start asking where the Superintendent in charge of the Gare de Lyon case has got to.'

'Talking of Germans, have you any news of my friend the Pink Potato?'

'The what? Oh, Schirach, you mean, of the German police. No, I haven't, but he must be up to something – I only wish we knew what.'

I'd have liked to spill the beans to the Superintendent just for once, but it was too late. I couldn't start now: I'd have to go on ploughing my lonely furrow. 'And in the meantime?' I asked.

'In the meantime none of the trails leads anywhere. The dancer, for example, has vanished, and heaven knows if we'll ever see her again.'

'We've put a man in her house,' ventured Bonvalet.

'Fat lot of good that's going to do us!' snarled Faroux. 'Still, never say die, eh? We've got a lot of stuff on Paul Clément – that'll be something, if we can nab him. With Maillard's murder to dangle over him we ought to be able to make him sing.'

'Oh, he'll talk all right, but will he tell you anything you want to know? He didn't look to me like one of the big shots.'

'That doesn't matter – he could lead us to the man you saw with him in the empty house. You thought that one was higher up the scale, didn't you? If we can't have the dancer we must get hold of him.'

A knock on the door heralded the arrival of the promised 'further details' on Clément. They were brought by a police clerk with a bureaucrat's stoop and a fierce local accent. After placing the papers on Faroux's desk, he hovered, obviously anxious to put his oar in.

'You'll notice, Superintendent,' he said, 'that at the time of the business at the chemicals factory, Paul Clément's half-brother André Clément was also a suspect. He's well known to us as a black marketeer, but we've never been able to catch him. A smart operator. He often goes to the Blackbird Club and various other disreputable places we've listed for you. And you'll be interested to learn that he's one of the cronies of the woman Barre, also known as Jackie Lamour.'

15 Even worse

Faroux swore loudly. I swore silently but more vehemently.

'We've got to get that man!' cried the Superintendent as he leapt from his chair, scattering objects right and left. The round-shouldered scribe seemed pleased with the effect he'd produced. Poking an inky finger at one of the papers he'd brought he murmured, 'This seems to be the address . . . Of course with these crooks one can't be sure—.'

'We'll go and have a look anyway!' interrupted Faroux. 'Fantastic! On your way, everyone! Step on the gas!'

'But sir . . . ' began Bonvalet.

'I know what I'm doing!' Faroux cut in. He was rubbing his hands gleefully, so happy he even told me I could go along.

'Th-thanks very much,' I gulped.

He looked at me in surprise. 'You sound as if I'd asked you to a funeral!'

In fact I was extremely miffed at the thought of Florimond Faroux collaring Dédé before I did. But yet again: what could I do but wait and see?

*

Out we went into the biting cold and drizzling rain, a night to match my mood. We piled into the police car and were whisked off by a driver from the local force. Faroux was still chortling at the prospect of laying hands on an important witness. His joyous exclamations made me feel distinctly green. He was about to cut the ground from under my feet without even knowing it. I must have had a long face, but as I was sitting right under a leak in the roof it looked as if my scowl was due to the involuntary shower-bath. Just as well – Faroux mustn't become suspicious. So far he didn't realize I was holding something back, something even I didn't dare to face. He'd have murdered me if he'd known.

Still, things could have been worse. If I hadn't been on the spot when the 'further information' on Paul turned up, Florimond and Co. could have found their man unbeknown to me. Now I'd discover whether my Dédé of Saint-Barnabé, the one who was waiting for Jackie to come back, really was the Pink Potato's contact. Faroux hadn't an arrest warrant and couldn't prove anything against him, so this whole expedition was going to end up either with a jawing match or with Dédé stuck briefly in the cells on some trumped-up charge and soon let out again. And then it'd be my turn to talk to him . . .

I lit my pipe, and though the tobacco was too damp from the rain for me to get a decent puff out of it, that didn't matter: I started to feel better. True, I was engaged in the most dangerous game of my career, and playing the ends against the middle in a way that could put everyone against me. And all because I had to solve every case myself, because I could never bear to tell the official police what I knew and then stand back and let them take it from there. It was a point of honour. Peculiar idea! Peculiar chap, Nestor Burma, I suppose – one can't change one's nature. But if I wanted to go on walking a tightrope over a precipice I'd need to keep a cool head: I must stop fretting and go back to the wait-and-see policy . . . My God, what wouldn't I give to be able to read the real message in those letters! Did Dédé know what they meant? Jackie must know, so must the Pink Potato. In the next few days I might have a chance to go to work on Dédé, but if he was our only link with Jackie and the Superintendent scared him off, we'd be done for.

It occured to me that old Florimond was forgetting the curfew.

'Sunset was ages ago, you know,' I said.

'What do you think I brought you along for?' he laughed. 'You can make yourself useful for once. You don't mind breaking curfew regulations, do you? *You're* going to call on André Clément first. You can see whether he's the man you heard talking to Maillard's killer, who may even be hiding out in the flat. If so, you've got to find a way to flush him or them out – after that, we'll take care of them.'

I couldn't refuse. Besides, although Florimond Faroux was being a bit high-handed, ordering Nestor Burma about, I wasn't sorry to be the first to meet Dédé face to face.

The street could have been worse and the building itself looked quite prosperous as far as I could see in the dark. The main door wasn't locked and we went straight in. The policemen stayed in the hall while I went off on my own to find the concierge. There was no answer to my knock on the lodge window: she couldn't be the conscientious never-off-duty type. At that moment someone found the time switch and the light came on, so I was able to see among the rows of mail boxes one marked *André Clément, 3rd floor right*. I climbed a dusty staircase with a clammy handrail, up to the door in question. I rang loud and long, I knocked and knocked, but nothing happened. There was nobody there. I wasn't all that surprised: Dédé didn't look like a man who went to bed at sunset, and when the Pink Potato had called two days earlier he was still not at home at a much later hour. Well, I thought, as Florimond was using me and had more or less given me carte blanche, I might as well make the most of it. I set about picking the lock: it didn't give me too much trouble.

It would have been quite a nice little flat if it hadn't been so untidy. A bottle of apéritif stood on the table beside a cracked ashtray and a pair of shoes. Dirty socks were draped on one of the chairs. The stove was clogged with what looked like hastily burned papers. I reached over to the shelf above the divan and tried the telephone. It was working.

After a swig from the bottle, I filled my pipe and took a look round. Dédé appeared to have cleared out. That was bad. I stirred the stove with the poker: there was nothing left but ash. As I straightened up I noticed, lying amongst all the muddle on the floor, a leather glove. I picked it up. The middle finger was damaged as if by a ring, and there was a stain on it that looked like blood. A label inside read 'Waldinger, Berlin'. Pocketing the glove, I went back to the phone.

I got through to the Moderne and asked to speak to Marc Covet. After a pause I was told he wasn't in. 'Could you give me M. Korb, please, room 109?'

'I'm sorry, sir, M. Korb is no longer here. He paid his bill this evening and left immediately.'

I said 'thank you' because it's the done thing in civilized society.

I went back downstairs to the policemen and was debriefed.

'What a bloody nuisance,' grumbled Florimond. 'He must have realized we'd get on to him through his half-brother and he's taken off. Since you've already had a look upstairs, Burma, we might as well do the same, warrant or no warrant. What have we got to lose?'

I led them up and we spent some time rummaging about in the flat and not finding a thing. As we were going out of the building we met a ferocious-looking old biddy coming in – the concierge coming home from the pictures, or from a grog with one of her chums. She eyed us suspiciously and demanded in a drinker's croak what we wanted.

'Police,' said Faroux. 'We're looking for one of your tenants, André Clément.'

'Does 'e always 'ave to 'ave 'is visitors at night?' she grumbled.

'How do you mean?'

'Come inside and talk. We'll catch our deaths out 'ere.'

Her cubby-hole smelt of onions and fug. A low-watt bulb shed a dingy pink light over all. I took what was left of a seat on a cane-bottomed chair, under a photo of a husband dead or fled.

'Got a fag?' she asked. Faroux offered to trade one for what she could tell us about her tenant. Gossiping, even with coppers, seemed to be right up her street, and she let herself go. From all the talk only two items of interest emerged. First, André Clément had had a caller two or three nights before, someone who made an awful noise banging about trying to find the light switch. She'd got up to see what was going on and the man asked which was André Clément's flat. Her description of this nocturnal visitor was not exactly lucid, and meant nothing to Faroux. I however recognized my old friend the Pink Potato. Second, the same man had been back this evening. At some stage a car had come to the door and André Clément had gone off in it with his visitor, telling the concierge he'd be gone two or three days and not to bother about his mail. That was a laugh! He hardly ever got any mail! He was carrying a case, and there might have been another on the seat of the car. When was this? About 7.30. Yes, 7.30 it must have been, just as she was going out.

All this confirmed my suspicions but didn't help us at all. The Superintendent drew up a plan of campaign for checking the mail, watching the building, inquiring at public places André Clément was known to frequent. But I wasn't hopeful. In my view we'd had it: we'd lost the trail, the case was collapsing, and I didn't like to think what had become of Marc Covet.

The worst, which was what I feared, hadn't happened: he'd only been beaten up. This I learned the next morning. Some time between eight and nine I was still lying in a daze on my palliasse at the sweet factory when Jean Rouget turned up, very amused about something.

'You're wanted on the phone,' he announced. 'It was ages before I could make out what the guy was trying to say – he seems to have some sort of speech impediment. He says his name's Covet, but it doesn't sound like Covet's voice to me. He tried to ring you last night at about 6.30, when you were out . . . '

I wasn't listening. I was already in Rouget's office, clad only in my shirt. I seized the phone.

'Hallo, Marc? My God, am I glad to hear you! I thought you were dead!'

' . . . Shtill a-ive . . . '

'What? it hurts you to speak, does it? Were you duffed up?'

'An' 'ow! . . . come . . . tell . . . '

'I'm on my way!'

I went and threw on my clothes and rushed off unwashed on a borrowed bicycle to the Moderne. I found Covet in his room, with a pink beard of sticking plaster round his jaw and one very black eye.

'This is Rote-Kartoffel's – alias the Pink Potato's – doing, isn't it?' There could be no doubt of it. He nodded. 'Out of the blue or because you were following him?'

'I suppose because I was following him.'

'I wonder why he didn't finish you off?'

The journalist's good eye flashed. 'Oh, very nice, very tactful! As usual!'

'Keep your hair on! Tell me how it happened.'

'The first time Korb went out I should have realized he was checking on me – just going a short distance to see if I'd follow, which of course I did. The next time we went much farther: he was looking for a lonely spot he could lure me to in due course, and he found one at the docks. On the way back to the hotel he stopped at a chemist's to buy the anaesthetic he was going to use on me. In the afternoon a worried-looking man came to the Moderne asking to see him.'

I gave him a brief description on Dédé: did it fit this caller?

'Exactly.'

'Good. Go on.'

But a violent sneeze made him groan, turn pale and swear volubly. 'He wasn't satisfied with just beating me up – he had to go and leave me lying in that filthy hole to catch pneumonia! It's agony when I sneeze!'

'I do sympathize,' I told him. 'But don't complain – he might have killed you or used his authority and had you sent to a concentration camp. It's funny he didn't.'

Marc gave me a dirty look. 'Some consolation! You seem to find all this very amusing!'

'I'm not joking.'

'Do you want to hear the rest of the story or not?'

'Come on then, spit it out.'

'After your friend Dédé had been, I tried to ring you at Allfruit, but you weren't there. Then Korb went out again and I followed him to the docks. It was getting dark and it was a dismal, evil-smelling place. Then all of a sudden, although I'd kept my distance, he was on me in a flash – I didn't have a chance. He was punching me in the face, with a knuckleduster, I think.'

'No,' I said, 'it was only a ring, but he hit you hard enough to split his glove.'

'I'm so glad to hear he had gloves on,' said Covet indignantly, 'I hadn't noticed! What would it have been like if he hadn't! Anyway, I came to I don't know how many hours later in a shed, in an icy draught, with the rain coming in and rats running about. And a splitting headache, not so much from the thumping as from the anaesthetic he gave me afterwards to keep me quiet. Don't ask me how I got back here – all I can remember is that I was fighting mad and wanted to go after the swine – I actually asked for him, but they told me he'd slung his hook.'

'Yes, he and Dédé went off together. They'll have

gone to join Jackie Lamour, wherever she is. Dédé must have had a message from her some time yesterday. Perhaps she's got what she wanted out of Victor Fernèse. So now, if you want to see a man who's come up against a brick wall, take a look at me.'

Tenderly Covet fingered his sore head. 'A brick wall's nothing! I bet it doesn't leave as many bruises as coming up against some fists I know!'

'Those bruises are the strangest part of the whole strange business,' I said thoughtfully. 'Here we've got a German cop who's also a cautious type, who writes notes to people in case they should be out when he calls, and prefers them to come and see him rather than telephone. And when he could get properly rid of someone who's being a nuisance, he merely gives him a good hiding! Not what you'd expect from a member of the Gestapo or whatever, is it? Of course, I'm pleased for your sake, chum, but for myself I'm wondering whether, as well as having all the trails dry up and not knowing what to do next, I didn't fail to see something that was right under my nose . . . '

'What d'you mean?' asked the journalist. He was still interested in the case in spite of the rough stuff involved. I looked at him, shrugged and held my peace. How could I tell him what I meant?

16 A little party

The barmaid poured some more of the pearly, illegal liquid into my glass and the water turned deliciously cloudy. Twenty-four hours had passed since Rote-Kartoffel and co. had driven off into the sunset. The worst hours of my life. While I was at my lowest ebb I'd found this nice little bar, and ever since I'd been pickling myself in pastis. The barmaid, who looked like a reader of novelettes, probably thought I was a disappointed lover drowning my sorrows, but I was only looking for inspiration. It hadn't worked. At this minute Jackie Lamour and her pals, if they hadn't yet got what they were after, must be giving Victor Fernèse a hard time somewhere. As I couldn't go and search the whole five hundred thousand square kilometres of France inch by inch, I sat here drinking. Perhaps the charming dancer would send me a postcard to let me know where she was.

Which reminded me, Hélène *had* sent me a card, to say all was well and no one had been bothering her. That was the only ray of sunshine in my existence at the moment, but it wasn't enough. It was some consolation to know that the combined efforts of the Sûreté and the Marseilles police hadn't been any more successful than mine. They were investigating André Clément's past and tracing his recent phone calls, but I was sure this would get them nowhere, and that the man they'd posted in Clément's flat would be as little use as the colleague kicking his heels out at Cap Croisette, hoping for a glimpse of Jackie Lamour's famous shanks. My view was that anyone round here wanting to see Jackie and Dédé would need a telescope. In short, friend Faroux was as stuck as I was: despite all his official apparatus he was going round and round in circles, followed by Bonvalet and Grégoire, for all the world like men in the Ripolin advert painting each other's backs. Normally I'd have chuckled at the thought, but not at the moment. Especially as it was possible the Superintendent was concealing as much from me as I was from him. Full cooperation, I don't think! I brought my fist down on the table and the girl, thinking I was calling her, hurried over with the bottle.

'The same again, sir?' She was beginning to get the idea.

'Yes, a nice stiff one,' I answered almost jovially. Suddenly hope was stirring again.

Ever since the start of the case I'd been swept along so fast by the giddy pace of events that I hadn't had time to observe priorities. Now, having no choice but to suspend my interest in certain other players in the drama, I could at last bring my mighty brain to bear on the Fernèse angle, too long neglected despite its supreme importance.

A visit to Saint-Gaudens was indicated.

I arrived there late the next afternoon, as the mountains cast their shadows through the dusk. I'd come by road via Carcassonne through the good offices of Jean Rouget, who had business contacts among the lorry-driving fraternity.

Saint-Gaudens itself was just like any other small provincial town, but once you got outside it things were different. Derricks loomed, reminding you of Mexico, except that here it was bitterly cold – I might as well not have bothered with my trenchcoat for all the good it did me.

I started off at a sort of shack, Hollywood gold-rush style, with a sign outside announcing very suitably that it was the office of the South-West Oil Company. The place was deserted except for a caretaker in the last stages of decrepitude: he could only just manage to articulate the name and address of the manager, who might be able to tell me what I wished to know about Victor Fernèse.

Back I traipsed into town, but when I finally found the right house the woman who came to the door told me what the silly old fool of a caretaker had omitted to mention – that the manager (presumably she was his wife or something) had been away for a couple of days and wouldn't be back for a couple more. Perhaps there was an assistant manager I could see? or an assistant assistant manager? M. Gautarel in the next street was, it emerged, just such a person.

He was a pleasant young man, but he'd only been here for a year and hadn't himself known the Victor Fernèse, engineer and former employee of the firm, after whom I was enquiring, I told him, on behalf of a client. However, he could put me on to someone else who *had* been here in 1939 and who'd spoken of Fernèse to him.

Fortunately, this contact could be effected only in a sort of barn where a numerous company gathered behind closed doors to imbibe various potations despite Marshal Pétain's strictures. The man who'd known Fernèse was no longer in his first youth, and was attempting to preserve himself in alcohol. M. Gautarel performed the introductions and withdrew.

When we'd moved to a table in a quiet corner, I ordered some white wine and started to question the old gent. Had he known Victor Fernèse? He certainly had! What he told me would have filled a telephone directory before the paper shortage. Only none of it was to the point. What I needed was someone who'd worked with him, shared his ideas, maybe listened to his confidences. This old soak couldn't help me. Did he know anyone who might? He shook his head dubiously as he poured another glass: there'd been so many transfers since the war. What about Matich – did he know the name? No. He was a friend of Fernèse's . . . foreign . . . Oh, did I mean the foreigner? But he wasn't a *friend* of Fernèse's, they only worked together! Friendship was something altogether different. If I wanted to know what friendship was . . . No thanks, I'd rather hear what he knew about Sdenko Matich. He didn't know anything, but to come back to the subject of friendship . . .

Did they sell anything stronger than wine here, I asked. (Having come all this way for nothing I might as well get drunk and forget my troubles.) The landlord's own concoction wasn't bad: would I like to give it a try? We both gave it a try. It was your genuine paintstripper – ingredients bought from the local oil company, I shouldn't wonder.

'Here,' mumbled the old boy, brightening suddenly after his umpteenth glass. 'I know who could tell you about the foreigner – perhaps Fernèse too, but certainly the foreigner, who lodged at his place. His name's Raoul and he keeps a little pub, the Relais du Bon Puits, a couple of kilometres from here on the Tarbes road. You could go and see him now, this evening – he's never in bed before two in the morning. He's from Toulouse, you see – these town people aren't like us. Shall I show you how to get there?' Dipping a gnarled finger in the rings left by the bottles, he drew a sort of map on the wooden table. 'You have to pass Fernèse's place to get to Raoul's. It wasn't much of a place when he lived there, but you should see it now!' He continued for a while in the same vein, but finally, having made sure I understood his directions, he let me go. I dragged my sloshed self out on to the dark road and set off towards the Relais du Bon Puits, hoping Raoul would let me have a bed for the night.

It was cold out – I was shivering in my thin raincoat. I was also hungry. I quickened my pace. Although the sharp wind was having a sobering effect I was lurching about on the rough surface of the road. Then the moon rose and I could see where I was going.

Before long I came to a tiny little house set back from the road on a rise in the ground. This must be where Fernèse had lived. It was a wretched sight standing there in the wan moonlight. Behind it skeletal derricks leaned like menacing monsters. It was there Victor Fernèse had made the fatal discovery which had led to so many violent deaths. And he a pacifist! What a frightful paradox!

Insensibly I'd been drawn towards the house. I passed what was left of a mail box fitted to a rotten post, its chipped name-plate dangling from a single nail: V   TOR RNESE. He at least had always used his real name. Dreamily – I was still well under the influence – I walked on until suddenly, somehow, I was inside the house. I walked down an L-shaped corridor. Turning the corner I stopped short and came back to earth with a bump. There was a shaft of light coming from a door left standing a few inches ajar.

I crept forward. Voices were coming from inside. If I put my eye to the crack I ought to be able to see quite a large section of the room.

I'd already sobered up a good bit: what I saw now speeded up the process. It would be completed by what I had coming to me.

Two smoky oil lamps shone dimly on the sparsely furnished room. I could see a rickety table, some packing cases, a cupboard fixed to one wall and a dirty, moth-eaten old armchair. On which, unshaven, wearing hat, overcoat and muffler, in command but clearly out of temper, sat Rote-Kartoffel. A second figure I recognized as Dédé was prowling up and down, casting multiple shadows across the room. He too was unshaven. His face was grey and, like the German, he looked angry. Crouching in a corner like a hunted animal was a third man, haggard, terrified, dressed in rags: Victor Fernèse.

'Your treatment's just a joke – it's never going to work!' said the German. 'You'd be better off accepting my offer. I shan't wait much longer. Mein Gott, why did I ever come here? I've had enough of camping out in the wilds, with no sleep and next to no food. One more day and then I'm leaving. You and your lunatic can just get on with it!'

'It's not up to me,' whined Dédé. 'And you know what she's like – she won't listen. She thinks she'll be able to get this clot's secret out of him, just like that, now she's re-created the conditions under which it was conceived, as she says. Bloody rot! it makes me sick!'

And I'm about to make you sicker still, my lad, I thought, reaching for my revolver.

I felt something press against my ribs. Could someone be trying my pipe trick on me? I rejected the theory as too optimistic, and I was right.

17 Pink potato or
   rare roast beef?

'Stick 'em up and get inside! And no funny business, moron!' hissed a female voice, and there followed a few choice expressions I won't repeat. Jackie's pretty lips could produce a style all their own. She kicked the door open. 'Visitors!' she announced.

Our entrance was quite effective. Dédé stopped dead in his tracks. Rote-Kartoffel tried to prise his heavy bulk out of the scruffy armchair. Were they surprised or were they surprised! Seen close to they looked really terrible. There was a soap shortage round here all right! The dancer was the worst of the lot, with her dress crumpled, her stockings wrinkled – one of them laddered – and her make-up worn off.

'I think we've met before, darling,' she said mockingly to me.

I had my hands in the air, I was caught like a rat in a trap – what a situation! But I had to keep my end up. 'It must have been in the red-light district,' I said.

'You lousy bastard!' She was beside herself with rage – I'd never have thought she was such a sensitive plant. When she lunged at me I was ready and knocked the gun out of her hand, at the same time giving her a terrific thump right in the famous bosom.

In other circumstances, of course . . . but now I hadn't the choice. As she staggered back, gasping and clutching her chest, I reached for my gun. A shot rang out, but I hadn't fired it. I felt a great thud on my arm, followed by a burning sensation. The force of the shot spun me round, and I saw Paul Clément standing in the doorway, a smoking pistol in his hand. The ruffian was paying me back for the hiding I'd given him at Saint-Barnabé: this was meant to be the first instalment. Helped by Dédé and Jackie, he fell upon me. They were all going at it like steam hammers – I thought I was going to be flattened! Earlier that evening I'd been longing for a lie-down, but this was ridiculous! I didn't think Rote-Kartoffel had joined in the slaughter – he didn't need to, the others were managing nicely – but I seemed to remember him moving the lamps out of harm's way. As we were battering away, the rumpus seemed to stir the mad chap into life. He started hollering, 'Lawrence! Lawrence! Formula 5! Formula 5!' It was heart-rending – more painful than the punches I was taking. And then I passed out.

Slowly, horribly slowly, I came back from the abyss. Alarm bells were ringing through the world. Either the whole of planet Earth was on fire or another war had broken out. I was out of it anyway – I didn't seem to have any arms or legs. The bells stopped and were replaced by a distant hum. Then I could make out a few words here and there, though they didn't mean anything. Gradually order returned. My head was swollen to three times its normal size and hurt more than my arm, which apparently had been bandaged. I was trussed up with wire which was cutting into my flesh. There was an argument going on. Cautiously I opened one eye.

Dédé was still pacing up and down. A dishevelled Jackie, her dress ripped in several places, I'm afraid, was sitting opposite Rote-Kartoffel, smoking a cigarette. Fernèse had gone, so had Paul, presumably guarding him. The trio were discussing the situation and taking no notice of me. I kept absolutely still, partly because it hurt to move and partly because I was in no hurry to become the centre of attention again. It was nice and peaceful like this.

As I lay there quietly watching, partly hidden by the table, my eye fell on one particular piece of paper, close to my face, amongst the rubbish on the dusty floor. The text was typed and in German. Slowly I moved my head so that I could painfully make out enough of it to guess the drift. It was headed *Nachforschungen und Untersuchungen, Petroleumgesellschaft,* that's to say the secret research and development section of the Petroleum Group. It instructed Agent M5 to contact . . . Dédé, probably . . . I also saw the German words for *agreement, purchase,* and *discovery* and lastly *Formula 5* in French.

The letter probably belonged to Rote-Kartoffel and must have fallen out of his pocket at some juncture. But I wasn't interested in how I'd come to see it. The important thing was that this was a secret 'read and destroy' document if ever there was one. But it hadn't been destroyed.

Already during my last meeting with Covet a curious thought had struck me. And this paper too . . .

'Hello, ducky! back in the land of the living, are we?' I'd been so wrapped up in my thoughts I hadn't noticed Jackie's approach. She underlined the question with a spiteful kick. 'So you're the famous Nestor Burma! That was a dirty trick you played on me, you swine! Stand him up, André, so that we can see his ugly mug.'

The thug seized me roughly and propped me against the wall all in one piece like an Egyptian mummy. Jackie slapped me to and fro across the face. I nearly fell over again!

'Now you're going to tell me exactly how you come into all this!' she raged. 'You thought you were so clever, didn't you, pinching the letters! Mucked things up properly for me, that did, and now you come poking your nose into my affairs again! All right, talk, blast you, and get a move on, or do I have to make you?' She was brandishing a pair of nail-scissors in front of my eyes – she would have used them, too, the crazy bitch.

'OK, OK,' I said meekly. 'Yes, I did take the letters. How was I to know you were so attached to them? Anyway, what do you expect? I'm no angel – I'm a private detective, I do what I'm paid to do. Well, this time after I've done the job I get the impression my client's tried to rub me out, so I go after him to have a few words on the subject. And I find *he's* been bumped off now as well. Well of course, that sort of thing always gives me a kick. So I started looking into the matter, partly because I'm a nosy parker and partly because I don't like being pushed around and made use of.'

She laughed scornfully and went over to the table, where the contents of my pockets had been spread out. 'Bernard didn't know,' she said, pointing to the banknotes, 'that he was ordering his coffin and yours. André, put this dough in my bag; it's better than nothing. And take this too.' She gave him my revolver. 'The size of it! You must be a big strong boy, Nestor, to lug that thing round in your pocket. A Spanish gun, eh? I'll keep it to remember you by.'

While she was keeping up this flow of taunts, Rote-Kartoffel had extracted himself from his chair and now, cold and silent, was going through my things, apparently choosing a trophy for himself. He examined my fountain-pen closely, scrutinized my papers and finally paused at a little red box which he picked up and started to toy with. I wondered what it was doing here. I should really have left it in Paris, but I must have forgotten and been carting it round in one of my pockets. It contained a close-up lens for my Rolleiflex. I hoped it hadn't been damaged in all that fighting, but when Rote-Kartoffel absent-mindedly opened the box I could see it was intact and still wrapped in its tissue paper. He closed the box and, still holding it, went back to looking at my documents. As the dancer continued to hurl insults at me, he looked me straight in the eye.

'A private detective, eh?' he said, but it wasn't really a question, and it was said with a strange look, a strange smile and a strange intonation.

I suddenly realized what a smart, alert, quick-thinking guy he was. My God, yes, *whoever he was*, he cottoned on fast! No wonder he rumbled Marc Covet almost as soon as he started being followed. But if he was so bright, how come he carried a secret document around with him instead of destroying it? Perhaps because he needed it to establish his identity. In which case *perhaps I should change the menu*? Instead of a Pink Potato, the Baron of Beef . . . the Roast Beef of . . . So I wasn't the only one who was deliberately risking his skin.

The fat man with the red face put my extra lens in the pocket of his coat and seemed to come to a decision.

'Now look here,' he said icily to the woman, 'I didn't come here to watch you having hysterics. That's enough nonsense – let's get on. Cards on the table. The letters have gone for good. And if you expect Fernèse to recover his sanity and tell us his secret just because he's back in the place where he discovered it, you must be as mad as he is. If he's going to be cured he needs proper treatment. I've made you an offer – it still stands. I can have him treated by a reputable psychiatrist. It's my last hope, though only a flimsy one. So I can hardly pay you what I was prepared to give for the letters themselves, containing all the details of the invention. Both sides will have to compromise. The sum I suggested—.'

'It's not enough!' she interrupted. 'I told you! What he's got in his head is worth millions.'

'Unfortunately I can't see inside his head. As things stand he's no use to us. My employers are the only ones who could get something out of him – they could try, anyway. Mein Gott, keep him if you like! You'll only have to kill him in the end to get rid of him, and you won't have had a pfennig's worth out of him. Whereas if you accept my offer . . . '

'What was the figure again?'

A heated argument followed over the sum involved. I listened to them going on and on, sometimes in whispers, the next minute shouting and swearing at each other, and all the time bargaining a man's life away. I would have been outraged if I hadn't known that in a way it didn't signify.

I must have been dozing, overcome with pain, fatigue and fever, when I was awakened by a hefty slap in the face. Jackie, wearing an overcoat on top of her ruined dress, was bidding me a fond farewell. Dédé and Paul were lined up behind her waiting for their turn.

The florid man in the loden intervened. 'That'll do,' he said. 'He and Fernèse both belong to me now. I told you I'd deal with him.'

Apparently the deal had been concluded. The hoodlums obeyed reluctantly and followed their lady boss out of the room, the fat man going too to see them off the premises. I heard their cars starting up behind the house, where they'd been concealed. When Rote-Kartoffel returned he was smiling.

'Alone at last!' he said with a sigh of relief. 'Now those cretins have cleared off we can have an intelligent conversation.'

He blew out the lamps and the smell of paraffin became more marked. Most appropriate. He opened the worm-eaten shutters, admitting a square of grey light. Dawn already! Coming over to me he untwisted the wire of my bonds, making me yell as he touched my injured arm.

'Ah, yes!' he said, 'you need a fresh dressing – something better than a handkerchief this time. Sorry, that's all I had last night.' He kicked the wires into a corner and brought my belongings over from the table in his cupped hands. 'Here's your stuff back, except for the revolver – I forgot to ask Mlle Lamour to return it. Oh, and this is yours too.' He handed me the little red box. I looked from it to him, my eyes gazing straight into his. I couldn't help saying admiringly, 'You're quick on the uptake, aren't you?'

'It's my job,' he answered.

Unsteadily I moved closer to this mysterious character. After a brief hesitation I decided to risk it. Now he'd seen through me I could show that I'd seen through him. 'I've been calling you Rote-Kartoffel, the Pink Potato,' I said. 'Shouldn't I change it to something like Rare Roast Beef, as in "The Roast Beef of Old . . . " '

'Very amusing!' he laughed. 'Yes, Rare Roast Beef

161

suits me nicely. It's more nourishing than spuds. But what made you suspect—.'

'There was a man tailing you and you wanted to get rid of him. You could have killed him, you could have had him arrested, but you didn't. Also . . . ' I held out the instructions from *Nachforschungen und Untersuchungen* to Agent M5. 'A real Gestapo officer wouldn't have spared my journalist friend. And the real Agent M5 would have destroyed this letter.'

'I admit I'm not Agent M5,' he said, taking the paper. 'This was delivered to the wrong address. The postman made a mistake. These things happen.'

I was feeling better. Now my wound had been cleaned and properly dressed my arm didn't hurt so much. And when he went to Saint-Gaudens for the dressings Roast-Beef had brought back food as well. He had an appetite that went with his nicknames and he could buy what he wanted – he had plenty of money. 'Very handy,' I said to myself; but I wasn't thinking of eatables.

After we'd consumed our cold meal we talked.

'Look at that poor man,' he said, nodding towards the corner where Victor Fernèse sat still and silent on a wooden crate. 'He really did invent a Formula 5. And the word got round to various secret services, because he approached several bodies about it. By the time they'd decided there was something in his invention and he wasn't just a madman, and the secret services were all falling over one another to lay their hands on it, it had disappeared, stolen by Sdenko Matich. And Fernèse *did* go mad. A whole web of secret agents spread all over the world to pick up any scrap of information that might lead to the recovery of the documents. It was no use. Sdenko Matich had vanished. I suppose it was from him that

Jackie Lamour got the letters. He must have found out she was in Marseilles and . . . You've heard of Charles Lantenant, of course?'

'The man who specialized in stealing secret documents?'

'That's the one. Jackie Lamour had been thick with him once and Matich must have known. As soon as the Croat came to Marseilles and offered her the Formula she realized its importance and got in touch with the *Petroleumgesellschaft*. They knew what it was worth too and Agent M5 was instructed to contact André Clément, who acts for Jackie in business transactions. And André Clément used to be Lantenant's second-in-command . . . '

Florimond Faroux must have known all this, I thought to myself. My friend the Superintendent must have been holding out on me, but I couldn't object – he was only paying me back in my own coin.

'As to why Matich didn't try to cash in the documents himself instead of letting Jackie have them, I suppose that after his trouble with the Gestapo he preferred to stay out of the limelight even if it cost him money.'

'Or perhaps he couldn't decode the letters,' I said.

'Nobody can.'

'What!'

'It wasn't by chance that there was a black ribbon tied round the packet. As it said in the paper addressed to Agent M5, it had been impregnated chemically with the key to the code used in the letters.'

My palms were moist with sweat. 'But it was lost in the fire at the Vieux Port!'

'That's right,' he said with a fatalistic shrug. 'The letters aren't so valuable without it. But people would still pay a lot to get hold of them.

'So, to get back to the story: Jackie Lamour contacts the *Petroleumgesellschaft* and their Agent M5 is supposed to come and wrap up the deal. But in the meantime things have been happening. A well-known private detective has stolen the letters from the dancer on behalf of an adventurer who'd got wind of them from her and realized he could make a fortune out of them. Matich gets mistaken for the thief and is killed. His body's discovered in Paris, where a certain person has joined the Gestapo precisely in order to try to trace him through the organization he used to work for. As soon as this certain person hears about the body in the train, he takes over the case himself. He's managed to become quite influential by now. In a while, when his mission's completed, it'll be different, I don't mind telling you. But for now he's got enough time and enough clout to see that you, M. Burma, get home safe and sound and without a stain on your character.'

'Thanks,' I said. 'I'm getting fed up with not being able to use my own name.'

'And I thought of you as modest!' he chuckled. 'Don't worry, your name'll be on everyone's lips when you explain your return from the dead. That'll be quite a job!'

'Oh, I know how to deal with journalists. It'll make a great story, but I've promised it to Marc Covet. And he's earned it!'

'Yes indeed . . . Now, after Matich's death this certain person I was talking about starts to keep an even closer eye than before on another individual who has connections with the pro-German intelligence branches of the Central European oil companies. As a result, Agent M5 never received this document.' He waved the paper I'd found on the floor. 'It's served its purpose now.' He struck a match and held the paper in the flame. 'But it was all I had to identify me to Jackie Lamour and Co. as Agent M5.' He ground the ashes into the floor with his heel. 'The rest you know.'

There was a short silence while I filled my pipe. 'Was it your idea to send men to my flat to arrest me?'

'It was. During the session at the Quai des Orfèvres it came out that you were a private detective, and I realized all that talk of secrecy was more likely to whet your appetite than to keep you quiet. I didn't want any interference, so I tried to get you put out of the way, and I wasn't fussy how. Sorry, but I'm no angel either. I was none too pleased when you gave us the slip.'

'Had you made the connection between my trip to Marseilles and Matich's death?'

'If I had I'd have questioned you about it right away. It would have saved me a lot of trouble.'

'Hm,' I growled sceptically. 'Of course, if you'd caught me you might have got out of me in Paris what you learned from me – if you did learn anything – here. But I might not have been so cooperative then. Although . . . As you said yourself, we're no angels, either of us. There were several times in Marseilles when I was on the point of coming to see you . . . By the way, did you recognize me at the Moderne?'

'I didn't even notice you. But you say you thought of coming to see me – why didn't you, then?'

'I was thinking of the future.'

'As always.'

'As always,' I agreed. 'And now, on the same principle . . . I told you I was feeling cooperative and it's true. Certain things you've said and done have made me revise my opinion of you. I've even envisaged a possibility which you haven't denied. But . . . I might have got it wrong. Both of us might. You find an extra lens, you pick it up, and you say to me, "A private detective, eh?" as if you were asking "Just a detective, is that all?" When you give it back to me, I simply remark, "You're quick on the uptake, aren't you?" It might have been an admission, it might not – I could supply another interpretation and then your theory about me collapses. And I've no more proof about you than you have about me.'

'You can never be too careful,' he agreed. 'That's why we've gone over the case working out the part played by this one and that one, but we've never once mentioned what it's really all about.'

'I need proof first,' I repeated.

'Listen,' he said, 'you've got a radio in Paris, haven't you? I'll come and have a drink with you one evening in your flat. Choose a message and a date – give me ten days because I've some business to attend to first – and I'll have the BBC broadcast it when I come. Would you accept that as proof?'

'Certainly.'

'Choose a message then.'

'Ghosts know no frontiers.'

His beefy cheeks quivered as he roared with laughter. 'Oh, very lyrical! So you're a poet as well!'

'As well as what?' I said.

18 Ghosts know no frontiers

Dastardly Dédé must have infected me with the fidgets: nervous Nestor, that was me. My pipe clamped between my teeth, I was pacing up and down my study. It was ten days since Roast-Beef had brought me back from Saint-Gaudens – ten days without news of him. Ten days without hearing any more from the German police, either – I took this as a good sign for the future. But still . . . I looked at the clock. In an hour's time I'd know which I was going to be: rich or hanged. In the second case, if my man was cleverer and more twisted than I thought, I might not be hanged out of hand but shot . . . eventually.

The radio was on with the volume low, emitting imitation jazz, Occupation jazz. I considered the set with mixed feelings: much depended on it for young Nestor. If my 'Ghosts' phrase was among the personal messages soon to be broadcast from London, I could expect to bring off a lucrative deal without any risk to myself. But where was Roast-Beef? He'd said he was going back to Marseilles, but by this time he should be on his way to my flat. I suddenly remembered Fernèse, and how decent Roast-Beef had been, getting him admitted to the Sainte-Anne mental asylum. As a permanent patient. Incurable. I was the only one now who could save the situation. I glanced at the leather briefcase I'd retrieved that day from my secretary's flat, where I'd left it the first time I came back from Marseilles. It was on that account I'd been so anxious about Hélène's safety when I was away being dead-and-alive.

The thought of the risks she'd been exposed to because of my peculiar morals made my head pound.

I opened the window. It was a cold night. The sky was bright with stars. But I didn't get the chance to look at it for long. A whistle shrilled. 'Put that light out!' yelled an air-raid warden. Poetry and war don't go together. I went back into the warm and went on with my thoughts, keeping up the fire in the stove and smoking pipe after pipe.

The doorbell rang. Roast-Beef stood on the landing. But he was not alone – Florimond Faroux was with him.

'Well, this *is* a surprise!' I exclaimed.

'I hope the Superintendent and the radio combined will do as a guarantee,' said Roast-Beef.

'Of course. Come in – there's a fire in the library.'

They sat down, but I remained standing with my hands in my pockets.

'You don't look very pleased to see us,' observed the secret agent.

'I don't like being made to look stupid. You two know each other, then?'

'We only met a few days ago. After Matich's death M. Faroux was entrusted with a certain mission – the French too were interested in Fernèse's discovery, you see. We've tended to see each other as competitors, but what with the war and our common struggle against the Nazis, we've come to an understanding, as M. Faroux will confirm.'

'You had something to hand over to this gentleman, Burma,' said the policeman.

'Yes, when we've heard the personal messages . . . A word in the meantime: Superintendent, there are a lot of things you knew that you didn't tell me. You weren't as much in the dark as you made out.'

'My job was simply to get as much information as possible about Matich and his connections, and that was all.'

'In this kind of work we have to play our cards close to our chest,' said Roast-Beef sociably.

I turned up the radio. 'London calling, London calling!' said a nasal voice.

'But you knew about Fernèse?'

'I knew he existed, and that the Croat had stolen the material about his invention.'

'At one point,' I said, 'I nearly mentioned him to Bonvalet, since he had connections with Saint-Gaudens. But I didn't. Just as well – you'd have realized I knew more than I was letting on, and things would have turned out differently.'

'And you have the cheek to accuse *me* of holding out on *you*!' fumed Faroux. 'How did you come to know Fernèse?'

I told him what had happened at the mental home. His moustache twitched.

'Well, well! You always manage to get a ringside seat whenever there's something going on! *I* only learned what happened at Ferdières when I got back here. As Delan was a friend of yours, you'll be glad to know his killer's been arrested. It wasn't one of Jackie Lamour's accomplices – just a hit man she hired for the job. He blabbed though, and that's how we caught him. I'd already been recalled to Paris by then and had received new orders. In particular I was told to come here tonight with this gentleman: he isn't really a member of the Gestapo, I'm glad to say.'

'That's what we're just going to—.'

'Here are the personal messages . . . ' said the radio. You could just make out the words through the jamming.

We held our breath and listened.

'The little girl's hat is a national treasure . . . Cleopatra will ride to the café on her bicycle . . . Special message: *Ghosts know no frontiers* . . . Repeat: special message: *Ghosts know no frontiers* . . . Don't let the children—.'

I switched off, went over to my briefcase, took out a roll of film and handed it to Roast-Beef.

'Here's a copy of the letters.'

'God Almighty!' gasped Faroux.

A smiling Roast-Beef was opening his own briefcase.

'All right, all right,' I said to Faroux. 'Don't swear and don't comment. Think what you like but don't say anything. It's bad enough your being here and seeing the trick I'm pulling. I'm not very proud of it, but damn it all,' I burst out, trying to hide my embarrassment beneath a show of anger, 'a man's got to live. I had the letters for a whole night, I knew they were supposed to be valuable, and there's always the future to think of – so I photographed them.'

'You're absolutely right,' said the man with the red face, who'd admitted he was no angel. 'Let's get this business over – I haven't got much time. As I explained earlier, M. Burma, the copy is worth less than the original letters because the ribbon with the key to the code is missing. Our cipher experts are going to have a lot of trouble breaking the code: but whether they succeed or not needn't concern you: I'm paying you for the copy. I have here a large sum of money, or rather half of it. You'll be paid the other half when the film's been developed and printed and we're certain it is what you say it is.'

He took several bundles of half-banknotes out of his briefcase and laid them out on the table.

'B-B-B died because of a note like those,' I said thoughtfully.

'Why don't you look on the bright side?' he answered. 'When you've got the other halves you'll be able to treat yourself to a dozen dancers twice as glamorous as Jackie Lamour. By the way . . . ' He burst out laughing. 'Something funny happened to her. At Saint-Gaudens I had to pay her a good round sum to get rid of her and be on my own with you. I intended to get it back afterwards, perhaps by having the Germans send her to prison. But by the time I got back to Marseilles she was in gaol already. When she went back to her place at Cap Croisette with Dédé and Paul, she ran straight into M. Faroux's men. I got my money without any bother by taking over her case and confiscating everything she had on her when she was arrested. Dédé and Paul are in prison down there, and they won't be out in a hurry, and she . . . ' He was laughing again. 'I handed her over to the Gestapo, saying it was to protect her from the French police, but really to give myself time to decide what to do with her. And guess what happened! The Germans discovered a gun in her handbag, a Spanish revolver they'd been looking for for some time in connection with the shooting of the Gestapo officer in the Vieux Port. What an extraordinary woman! I couldn't do anything for her of course, disapproving as I do of that kind of murder. So . . . A pity really – she used to have such a pretty figure. It can't have looked very charming with a dozen bullet holes in it.'

Faroux and Roast-Beef must have only just got downstairs when the air-raid warning went. It didn't even occur to me to go down to the shelter – I was overwhelmed by a

wave of lassitude and depression. The bisected banknotes
still lay on the table. I'd put them away tomorrow, I
thought. Unless a bomb . . . As if on cue an enormous
explosion shook the building to its foundations. It might
save me money in the long run, having that bloody
factory down the road. I wouldn't have to buy a flag
to celebrate the end of the war – I wouldn't be there! I
still didn't think of going down to the cellar. Everything
seemed utterly futile. I sat down.

The stove was roaring away. So were the planes
overhead. I heard a door open and the sound of my
neighbour going down to the shelter with her baby. It was
crying. I remembered that B-B-B had been a baby too,
and Maillard, and Jackie Lamour, and all the people who
were going to die that night and on other nights, people
called Smith and Müller and Dupont. Nerves stretched
to breaking-point, I waited for the next explosion, not
sure whether I wanted or feared it. It didn't come. All I
could hear was some strange thuds in the distance. Then
came the sharp crack of an anti-aircraft gun close by. In
the ensuing silence a church clock chimed, each hour
dropping peaceably into the surrounding atmosphere
of dread, increasing the tension by the contrast. Time
continued to pass. This always amazes me. I looked at
the clock on the mantelpiece, ticking away as if nothing
had happened. My visitors had been gone five minutes.
I found it hard to believe.

The doorbell rang. I started, then went to answer it
as if in a dream. Florimond Faroux almost fell into my
arms. The sight of him brought me back to my senses.

'Good God!' I cried. 'Look at the state you're in!
What happened?' He was bareheaded, his clothes were
torn and singed, and a streak of blood ran across one
cheek and down on to his moustache.

'It's nothing,' he panted. 'I might have been killed.'
He collapsed into an armchair and passed a dirty hand
over his eyes. 'Have you got anything to drink in the
house? That's what I came back for. My God, what
a shock! It happened about half a mile from here. A
terrible racket, and then the car and everything went
flying. I thought the whole street had gone up with us. I
don't know how I got out – perhaps because I'm thinner
than he was . . . '

I put two glasses on the table among the bundles of
notes and filled them with black-market brandy. 'Oh,'
I said, 'so he . . . ?' I took a gulp of brandy. Faroux
followed suit.

'Like a torch, Burma, like a torch. His last thought
was about his mission. "The film!" I heard him scream.
But it went up in flames too – there was nothing I could
do about it.'

His hand trembled as he poured himself another drink.
The bottle clinked against the glass. I shook my head,
lit my pipe. Outside, the night shuddered at the shock
of distant explosions. I stared at the bundles of half-
notes.

'The film!' breathed Faroux. Then: 'You're a peculiar
bastard, Burma!'

'I suppose so,' I said. I couldn't take my eyes off the
money. Then I shrugged. 'And being a peculiar bastard
is like crime . . . or war . . . '

I took a bundle of notes and, opening the stove,
began to feed them one by one into the fire.

'It doesn't pay.'

Paris 1946

The Rats of Montsouris £3.99

'Then, slowly, without quite knowing why, I retraced my steps. Was it because of the redhead or because of the man with the tattoo? I think on the whole, it was because of the redhead . . . '

A rendezvous with a fellow ex-POW leads Nestor Burma, dynamic chief of the Fiat Lux Detective Agency, to a dimly lit bar in the rue du Moulin-de-la-Vierge. A venue quite empty of both windmills and virigns . . .

What he finds there is his tattooed mate, now part of a gang of burgulars called the Rats of Montsouris. But this particular Rat is on to something so big he can only trust Burma. And when someone betrays him, the question remains - what *are* the back streets of the 14th arrondissement hiding?

Burma, assisted by the beautiful Hélène, is in for a string of seedy surprises . . .

All Pan books are available at your local bookshop or newsagent, or can be ordered direct from the publisher. Indicate the number of copies required and fill in the form below.

Send to: **CS Department, Pan Books Ltd., P.O. Box 40, Basingstoke, Hants. RG21 2YT.**

or phone: 0256 469551 (Ansaphone), quoting title, author and Credit Card number.

Please enclose a remittance* to the value of the cover price plus: 60p for the first book plus 30p per copy for each additional book ordered to a maximum charge of £2.40 to cover postage and packing.

*Payment may be made in sterling by UK personal cheque, postal order, sterling draft or international money order, made payable to Pan Books Ltd.

Alternatively by Barclaycard/Access:

Card No.

Signature:

Applicable only in the UK and Republic of Ireland.

While every effort is made to keep prices low, it is sometimes necessary to increase prices at short notice. Pan Books reserve the right to show on covers and charge new retail prices which may differ from those advertised in the text or elsewhere.

NAME AND ADDRESS IN BLOCK LETTERS PLEASE:

Name

Address

3/87